USA Today bestselling au wildly popular archaeolo former Navy SEAL tu Maddock!

There is a world beyond the one we know. And we are not welcome there.

Finding the burial site of Hawaii's greatest king is only the beginning for former Navy SEAL turned treasure hunters, Dane Maddock and Bones Bonebrake. When a pagan cult sets its eyes on the legendary Treasure of Eden, it's up to Maddock and Bones to get there first. But to reach the fabled land, they must first solve one of history's most confounding riddles and find the lost tomb of Alexander the Great!

Wood expertly blends history, myth, and legend in this action-packed adventure!

Classic adventure for the modern reader! Fans of Indiana Jones, Dirk Pitt, and Doc Savage will love the Dane Maddock Adventures!

PRAISE FOR DAVID WOOD AND THE DANE MADDOCK ADVENTURES!

"What an adventure! A great read that provides lots of action, and thoughtful insight as well, into strange realms that are sometimes best left unexplored." Paul Kemprecos, author of Cool Blue Tomb and the NUMA Files

"Dane and Bones.... Together they're unstoppable. Rip roaring action from start to finish. Wit and humor throughout. Just one question - how soon until the next one? Because I can't wait." Graham Brown, author of Shadows of the Midnight Sun

"David Wood has done it again. Within seconds of opening the book, I was hooked. Intrigue, suspense, monsters, and treasure hunters. What more could you want? David's knocked it out of the park with this one!" Nick Thacker- author of The Enigma Strain

"A twisty tale of adventure and intrigue that never lets up and never lets go!" Robert Masello, author of The Einstein Prophecy

"A page-turning yarn blending high action, Biblical speculation, ancient secrets, and nasty creatures. Indiana Jones better watch his back!" Jeremy Robinson, author of SecondWorld

"With the thoroughly enjoyable way Mr. Wood has mixed speculative history with our modern-day pursuit of truth, he has created a story that thrills and makes one think beyond the boundaries of mere fiction and enter the world of 'why not'?" David Lynn Golemon, Author of the Event Group series

"Let there be no confusion: David Wood is the next Clive Cussler. Once you start reading, you won't be able to stop until the last mystery plays out in the final line." Edward G. Talbot, author of 2012: The Fifth World

"I like my thrillers with lots of explosions, global locations, and a mystery where I learn something new. Wood delivers! Recommended as a fast paced, kick ass read." J.F. Penn, author of Desecration

"The literary equivalent of the theme park roller coaster!" BookAnon

Eden Quest- ©2022 by David Wood

The Dane Maddock Adventures™

All rights reserved

Published by Adrenaline Press
www.adrenaline.press

Adrenaline Press is an imprint of Gryphonwood Press
www.gryphonwoodpress.com

This is a work of fiction. All characters are products of the author's imagination or are used fictitiously.

ISBN: 9798825841076

BOOKS BY DAVID WOOD

THE DANE MADDOCK ADVENTURES
Blue Descent
Dourado
Cibola
Quest
Icefall
Buccaneer
Atlantis
Ark
Xibalba
Loch
Solomon Key
Contest
Serpent
Eden Quest

DANE AND BONES ORIGINS
Freedom
Hell Ship
Splashdown
Dead Ice
Liberty
Electra
Amber
Justice
Treasure of the Dead
Bloodstorm

DANE MADDOCK UNIVERSE
Berserk
Maug
Elementals
Cavern

Devil's Face
Herald
Brainwash
The Tomb
Shasta
Legends
Golden Dragon
Destination: Rio
Destination: Luxor
Destination: Sofia

JADE IHARA ADVENTURES (WITH SEAN ELLIS)
Oracle
Changeling
Exile

MYRMIDON FILES (WITH SEAN ELLIS)
Destiny
Mystic

BONES BONEBRAKE ADVENTURES
Primitive
The Book of Bones
Skin and Bones
Lost City
Alamo Gold

JAKE CROWLEY ADVENTURES (WITH ALAN BAXTER)
Sanctum
Blood Codex
Anubis Key
Revenant

BROCK STONE ADVENTURES
Arena of Souls
Track of the Beast

Curse of the Pharaoh (forthcoming)

SAM ASTON INVESTIGATIONS (WITH ALAN BAXTER)
Primordial
Overlord
Crocalypse

STAND-ALONE NOVELS
Into the Woods (with David S. Wood)
The Zombie-Driven Life
You Suck
Callsign: Queen (with Jeremy Robinson)
Dark Rite (with Alan Baxter)

WRITING AS FINN GRAY
Aquaria Falling
Aquaria Burning
The Gate

WRITING AS DAVID DEBORD

THE ABSENT GODS TRILOGY
The Silver Serpent
Keeper of the Mists
The Gates of Iron

The Impostor Prince (with Ryan A. Span)
Neptune's Key

A NOTE FROM DAVID

I rarely tell the story we all "know." As a reader and a writer, I don't enjoy the sort of story that takes us down the familiar path to a conclusion we all know is coming. I like lots of twists, and this book is no exception.

None of the above will be any surprise to a veteran Dane Maddock reader. Unfortunately, I do receive the occasional email from a reader who accuses me of "attacking the Bible" or "unintentionally leading people away from the truth." So, here's my disclaimer.

This is a fun adventure novel. It's neither a work of theology nor history. Any spins I put on Biblical or historical figures and stories is purely for fun. If you don't like that kind of story, you have been warned.

But if you're a reader who loves twists, turns, and surprising spins, I think you're going to love *Eden Quest*!

Happy reading!

David

*The Lord God planted a garden toward the east, in Eden;
and there He placed the man whom He had formed.*

Genesis 2:8

1

Dane Maddock breathed in the crisp morning air and let the sound of the rolling surf wash over him. The beach was empty, all was quiet. He was an early riser, and Lanai, the smallest of the publicly accessible Hawaiian Islands, drew very few tourists. He had the place to himself and that was all right by him.

His feet pounded the soft sand as he ran toward the sunrise that painted streaks of orange on the horizon. He tasted the salt air, drank in the gentle sound of the surf.

"I could get used to this."

He was enjoying a free stay at a beachfront resort, courtesy of his girlfriend, Spenser Saroyan, who was a travel journalist and social media influencer. She had been offered a free trip for two in exchange for reviewing the resort and its amenities. She had placed a particular emphasis on the number two. Bones, Maddock's best friend and partner in their treasure hunting business, was not invited. Neither was Spenser's twin brother Dakota, whose softness of heart was matched only by the softness of his brain. But even in his absence, Bones was screwing up Maddock's relaxing vacation.

"Why did he have to tell me about the lost tomb just as I was leaving?" Maddock said to the sky. "He knows that's all I'll be thinking about."

He heard the cry of a seagull. No, that couldn't be. There were no seagulls in Hawaii. He shook his head and kept running.

The cry came again and this time he recognized it. Someone was in trouble.

He remembered something he had read in the news. There had been a rash of disappearances among the homeless population of the local islands. Was he hearing a crime in progress?

"Help me!" It was a young woman's voice. He panned the

horizon and spotted a head bobbing just above the surface of the ocean just beyond the breakers.

He dashed into the frigid water until he could run no further, then he began to swim. He quickly closed the distance between them.

Twice the girl went under but fought her way back to the surface. She was gasping, choking. He remembered the old saying- "The third time a swimmer goes under they don't come back up again."

"Hold on!" Maddock shouted. "I'm almost there."

The girl tried to call back, but water filled her mouth. Gagging and sputtering, she sank beneath the surface again.

Maddock poured everything he had into the effort. In seconds, he had reached the spot where she had disappeared. He took a breath, blew it out, and plunged beneath the water.

The saltwater burned his eyes, and the early morning light visibility was nil. He spotted her just a few meters below him, her black hair spread out around her like a halo.

With a few strong kicks he reached her. He wrapped his arms around her chest and swam for the surface. She was surprisingly heavy considering the size of her frame, which was small. She was muscular, probably an athlete of some sort.

Finally, they broke the surface and the girl sucked in a deep breath and began to struggle. As a former Navy SEAL Maddock was experienced in water rescues. Swimmers in danger of drowning tended to panic, fight, and often drag their rescuer down with them.

"Float on your back," he said in a voice of command. His tone startled her, and she froze for a split-second. "I'll support your weight and make sure you float. You concentrate on breathing."

It worked. Her struggles ceased and she permitted Maddock to take her into shallow water.

"Thank you." She was breathing heavily but otherwise seemed to be okay.

"Can you walk?" he asked.

"I think so. I'm really tired."

Maddock helped her stand. Her knees wobbled and she grabbed hold of him.

"I guess I'll need your help a little bit longer," she said.

"No problem. You got a name?" he asked as he helped her to shore.

"Larkspur, but you can call me Lark," she said.

"I'm Dane, but everybody calls me Maddock."

"I think I can walk on my own now," Lark said when they were ankle-deep in water. She released her vice grip on his arm and turned to face him.

It was the first good look at her Maddock had gotten. She had creamy skin, full lips, jet black hair, and eyes that were deep violet in color. He didn't know if he would call her beautiful, but her appearance was striking.

"Dane Maddock, you are my hero." Lark wrapped her arms around his neck and hugged him tight. Damn, she was strong!

"All in a day's work," he said.

"Don't sell yourself short. Not many people are willing to so much as inconvenience themselves, much less risk their lives, to help someone else." She kissed him on the cheek. "I'm really sorry to have to do this." Her voice was a husky whisper.

"Do what?"

Maddock felt a sharp sting over his shoulder blade. He shoved Lark away, sending her tumbling into the water. He reached back and his fingers closed around a small cylinder. He could tell immediately what it was. With a sharp sting of pain, he tugged the needle free.

"What was in here?" He held up the syringe.

"Nothing that will hurt you." Lark scrambled backward on all fours like a crab. "It will just make you sleep for a little while."

"Why?" Maddock took a step toward her, but already he felt like he was walking in wet cement.

"We need your help. If you cooperate, you and Spenser will be free to continue your vacation. You will never hear from us again."

Maddock's heart skipped a beat. If these people, whoever they were, had taken Spenser, he would take the world apart to find her.

"Don't worry. She is safe, but she's under supervision until you provide us with the help we require." Lark was backing away, keeping a safe distance between herself and Maddock. "Like I said, do what we ask, and nobody gets hurt."

"What do you want with me?" His mouth was dry and his tongue felt thick.

"We need your expertise. It's a project that's right up your alley. You might even enjoy it."

"Why not just ask me?" His legs were wobbly, and he could scarcely keep his feet.

"I don't know the full story, but you and the boss have a complicated past. I have to admit, she was right about you. You jog at a ridiculously early hour, and you can't resist a damsel in distress."

The light was fading. His field of vision shrank to tiny circles. Maddock wobbled and sank to his knees in the soft sand.

"Who is your boss?" he mumbled.

Lark fixed him with a pitying smile.

"You'll meet her soon enough."

2

The Ford Bronco came bounding up the road, loud music announcing its approach long before Koa saw it. The vehicle appeared out of the jungle in a blur of red and skidded to a halt in front of the guard hut and the locked gate that blocked the dirt road.

"What the hell?" Koa shouted, stalking toward the vehicle. "You're going to kill somebody driving like that!" He froze when the driver's window rolled down and a dark-haired, purple-eyed woman stuck her head out.

"You don't like my driving?" Lark asked, a cloying smile on her face.

"Not especially," Koa said. He never knew what to make of the young archaeologist. Lark was impossible to work with, overbearing, even a bully at times. But she was also a flirt, quick to pinch his butt or plant a quick kiss on his cheek when no one was looking. She was an enigma.

Lark stuck out her lower lip, made a pouty face. "Aren't you going to open the gate for me?"

Koa tensed. In Hawaiian, his name meant Bold Warrior. Right now, he felt anything but that. He was just a lowly security guard. Why had they left it to him to deliver the news?

"I can't let you in," he said.

"Did you lose the key?"

"You are off the job. The university will be taking over the project starting tomorrow. I'm not supposed to let anyone else in."

Lark cut the engine and climbed out of the Jeep. The other doors opened, and two more people exited. He recognized them as Hunt and Tama, bouncers from a local bar who occasionally moonlighted as collectors for local drug dealers. Hired goons.

"We are on the verge of discovery and now the government wants to take over. What a surprise," Lark said.

"Don't kill the messenger." Koa forced a laugh. No one else

joined in.

"Trust me, Koa," Lark said. "You don't want to get in the middle of this."

"I'm just doing my job," Koa said with a confidence he didn't feel. He could handle himself in a fight, but one of the bouncers alone would be as much as he could deal with.

"Would you do it for me? Please?" Lark batted her eyelashes.

Koa swallowed hard and shook his head. Good jobs were hard to come by in the islands. If he lost this one, it was back to minimum wage and no benefits.

"That's too bad." Lark drew a pistol and took aim at Koa. "This is why I didn't become a veterinarian. I hate putting down pets."

Koa's head swam. What was she saying? He reached for his can of mace, fumbled with the Velcro strap that held it in place.

"No!" Koa raised his hands and backed away.

Lark thrust out her lower lip in a sad pout as she squeezed the trigger.

When Maddock came to, he was lying on the back floorboard of an old Ford Bronco. His wrists were cuffed, his ankles shackled, and he was lying on his back, knees pressed against his chest. He heard voices, a shout, and then a gunshot. Moments later the passenger door opened.

Maddock found himself staring up at a burly man with long hair. Tribal tattoos marked his arms. He grinned.

"The little baby woke up."

Maddock kicked the man full in the face. He felt the solid impact of his heel on the bridge of the man's nose.

With a roar of anger, the man reeled away, hands pressed

to his face. When they came away, blood streamed from his broken nose.

"You'll pay for that," he growled.

"Leave it, Hunt," Lark ordered. "The boss doesn't want him injured."

"Look at what he did to me!" Hunt protested.

"When you handle a venomous snake, you do it with care. Same goes for dangerous humans. Otherwise, you might get bitten." Lark shoved the big man out of the way and helped Maddock out of the cramped space.

Maddock looked around. They were in the jungle. In front of them, a security gate barred a dirt road that disappeared into the trees up ahead.

"Where are we?" he asked.

"The boss will tell you what she wants you to know." Lark took him by the elbow and gently but firmly guided him toward the gate, which one of her underlings, another big man, was unlocking. The body of a uniformed security guard lay nearby, shot through the heart.

"What did he do wrong?" Maddock asked.

"He did not cooperate."

"That doesn't bode well for me. I'm not the obedient type," Maddock said.

"You served in the armed forces, which means you are capable of following orders when necessary," Lark said. "It would be in your best interest to do so now. There really is no need for violence." She cast a meaningful look at Maddock, who knew exactly what she meant. Spenser's life might depend on his cooperation.

"All right, but make it quick," he said. "I haven't had my morning coffee yet, and it makes me grouchy."

Lark smiled coyly. "We can't have that now, can we?"

While Hunt stayed behind to dispose of the body and secure the gate, Lark and the other goon, a man named Tama, escorted Maddock through the jungle to the base of a sheer, volcanic cliff. Hidden by dense vegetation was a cleft in the rock. They squeezed through until it opened into a narrow passageway.

As Lark guided them through a series of twists and turns, Maddock made a mental note of each turn they took, every spot where the tunnel branched off, so that he was confident he could find his way back out again. Finally, they came to a spot where a rope and pulley were set up above a deep pit. The counterweight, a large boulder, dangled over the open space.

"Headquarters is down there," Lark said.

"Do I ride down on that?" Maddock asked.

"I could give you a push if you prefer." Lark grinned, winked.

Tama silently pointed to a ladder. They climbed down in silence. At the bottom of the pit stood a folding table. Maps, papers, books, and a laptop sat atop it. A small portable generator provided power to a pair of electric lights. On the opposite side of the pit, a passageway was roped off. Maddock moved to the table and examined the papers. He recognized the subject matter immediately.

"What is going on here? How long have you people been manipulating me?" He picked up the sheaf of papers and shook them at Lark.

"I don't know what you're talking about." Lark's face was a mask of innocence.

"You're looking for the lost tomb of Kamehameha. Three days ago, just before my flight to the islands, I got an email from a friend about this same subject. You're telling me that's a coincidence?"

Kamehameha I, or Kamehameha the Great, was the founder and first ruler of the Kingdom of Hawaii. The location of his final resting place was one of the Hawaiian Islands' greatest mysteries.

"I'm afraid I am the one at fault." The voice came from the direction of the tunnels.

Maddock turned to see a familiar face. One he had hoped to never see again.

"You have got to be kidding me."

3

A beautiful woman, tall with auburn hair, creamy skin, and eyes of deep green, stood before him. She bit her lip and forced a nervous half-smile. Maddock had cared for her once. And then she had betrayed him.

"You're the boss?" Maddock said bitterly.

"Well, I'm no Bruce Springsteen, but that's what they call me." Isla Mulheron forced a grin which immediately evaporated beneath the heat of Maddock's glare. "I was afraid of this."

"You stole from me and left in the middle of the night," Maddock said. "Bones was right. I should have learned my lesson the first time you screwed me over."

"I don't suppose it would make any difference if I told you I traded that stolen artifact for your life. They were going to kill you and Bones."

"You should have told them to get in line," Maddock said. "You set me up, you kidnapped me, and you've threatened the woman I love. You have no credibility with me."

Isla winced. Maddock's words had obviously wounded her.

"I needed your help, and I knew you wouldn't come if I asked you. So, I arranged a free vacation for you and your girlfriend. I knew you'd go for a run early in the morning when no one else would be out, and we planned accordingly. I even spoofed Bones' email address and sent the information about Kamehameha. I knew it would spark your interest." She smiled knowingly. "You've already been researching it, haven't you?"

"You don't know me as well as you think," Maddock grumbled. "And there's no way in hell I'm going to help you."

"Dammit, Maddock, stop wasting time!" Isla slammed her palm down on the table. "You and I both know that in the end, you are going to help me because you won't risk Spenser's life." She lowered her voice. "I have never wanted to be at odds with you. I swear it."

"How can I trust you?" Maddock said.

Isla turned to Lark, and with a flick of her fingers sent her to the far end of the cavern. Next, she took a key from her pocket and calmly freed Maddock from the cuffs and shackles.

"Thanks," he said, rubbing his wrists. "Wasn't easy descending the ladder with those on."

"I knew you'd be up to the task. You always are." Isla blushed, looked down at her feet.

"Are you sure you want to send your guards away?" Maddock said.

"I don't think you'll kill me. And I've got Lark to watch my back." She rubbed her hands together. "Shall we get down to business?"

Maddock saw no immediate way out of the situation, so he decided cooperation was best. He'd keep his eye open for a way out.

"What does the Tuatha want with Kamehameha's tomb?" he asked.

The Tuatha de Dannan was an underground organization much like the Illuminati. They took their name from Celtic tradition. Isla's mother was the leader, and she had chosen loyalty to the Tuatha over Maddock.

Isla hesitated. "There's something buried with him. That's all I can tell you."

"Fine. What's the status of the dig?" he asked as he flipped through the notes and charts. Most of it was information with which he was already familiar, thanks to Isla's phony email. The rest were maps of a system of tunnels.

"We're most of the way there," Isla said. "I'm hoping you can help us clear the final hurdle." She turned and called out to her underlings. "Lark, come with us. Tama, you stand guard here. Don't let anyone in or out without my say-so. Especially not anyone from the university."

Isla took the lead with Lark bringing up the rear. She led them through a series of twists, turns, and tight squeezes. She pointed out passageways she and her team had already explored.

"It's been slow going up to this point," she said. "And now that we're on the precipice, the university wants to take over. They've been dropping hints for a few weeks. That's why I pressed you into my service. The clock is ticking."

"What makes you so certain you're even on the right track?"

Isla turned and smiled. "I'll show you."

4

They squeezed through a narrow cleft in the volcanic rock and emerged into a chamber lit by battery-powered lamps. Maddock drew in a sharp breath. The walls were covered in relief images of deities and guardians out of Polynesian religion. At the center of the chamber lay a rectangular-shaped slab of gray rock. Maddock crinkled his nose. There was a faint, acrid smell in the air that he couldn't quite place.

"We call this the Room of Snares," Isla said, as if that explained the odor. "That slab in the center is a replica of the Naha Stone," she continued. "It was used to prove the true bloodline of the Naha Clan, a bit like the legendary Sword in the Stone. When a boy was born, his father would set him atop the Naha Stone. If he remained silent, his bloodline was true. If he cried, he would be cast out."

Maddock nodded. He was familiar with the legend.

"We've identified all the carvings, too."

"How did you ever find this place?" he asked, thinking of the many twists and turns they had made along the way.

"Kamehameha's body was hidden by his two most trusted friends, Hoapili and Hoʻolulu. Years later, the king's great-grandson, Kamehameha III, persuaded Hoapili to show him the way to the tomb. Hoapili let him to the pit, but he would proceed no further. He claimed he could no longer remember the safe path beyond that point."

"What about the markings on the floor?" Maddock said. Here and there were small, shiny dots.

"Stars," she said. "We think they represent the night sky at the moment of Kamehameha's birth. You can take a closer look. Just don't touch the walls. You'll get zapped."

Maddock realized what he had smelled earlier. The sickening smell of burnt human flesh.

"You've lost people?"

"Only a few of our own," Lark interjected. "We've mostly brought on contractors to identify the booby-traps, tunnels that collapse, floors that fall out from under you, that sort of thing."

"What kind of contractor does that?" Maddock asked, making a slow circuit of the room, and inspecting each relief sculpture.

"The kind that won't be missed," Lark said.

"Are you the cause of the recent wave of disappearances among the homeless?" Maddock asked. Lark shrugged indifferently.

"That wasn't my decision," Isla said. "The Tuatha are working with another organization. They are much more powerful than we, and they have some very specific beliefs about certain classes of people."

"That's disgusting," Maddock said.

"It's done and dusted, so no point arguing about it now. Unless you're ready to call off our deal."

Maddock bit back a sharp retort. As long as Spenser was under his captor's thumb, he had to play along. He racked his brain, trying to remember all he had read about the legendary king.

According to traditional local beliefs, people possessed mana, a sort of spiritual energy related to forces of nature, such as wind, thunder, and lightning. Kamehameha the Great was said to have been a divine child, born with an abundance of mana, and accumulating it at a prodigious rate during his lifetime.

"Wind, thunder, and lightning," he said aloud.

"Way ahead of you," Isla said. "Haikili, the god of thunder, is represented over there." She pointed across the room. "Touch anywhere on her surface and you get a deadly shock. Same with Kaha'i, demigod of thunder and lightning." She pointed to another figure. "And then there's

Paka'a, god of the wind. Touch him and he blasts you with poison gas."

Maddock scratched his head. "Kamehameha the Great was associated with Kū, the god of war. I suppose you've tried that one?"

Isla nodded. "A trapdoor sprang open and dropped Lark's 'contractor' into a lava pit. The other images on the wall seem to be benign. They don't trigger any traps, but neither do they open anything or appear to hold any secrets."

"What's that figure over there?" Maddock pointed to the stylized image of a reptilian warrior bearing a shining spear.

"We believe that is Waka, the lizard goddess," Isla said.

Maddock had seen artistic representations of Waka before, and she bore no resemblance to this figure. It was humanoid, with reptilian scales and a flat nose.

"You sure about that?" he asked.

"It might be one of the other lizard deities. But I know for certain that it's only a statue. No traps."

Maddock had a feeling she was hiding something, but he let it drop for the moment. He looked down at the floor, stamped his foot.

"Any hollow spaces?"

"Only the trapdoor that leads to the lava. Everything else appears to be solid, including the ceiling." Isla glanced up. "We even tried moving the Naha Stone, but it won't budge."

That left the star pattern on the floor as the only possible clue. Maddock knelt and ran his fingers across the constellation at his feet. The stars that made up the constellation Orion had been melted into the rock, leaving a glossy sheen on the surface. They sparkled when the beam of his flashlight passed over them.

"What celestial objects are associated with Kamehameha?" he asked.

"Only Halley's Comet, but it's not represented here." Isla heaved a tired sigh. "So close, yet so far away. Who knows where the bones are hidden?"

"That's it!" Maddock sprang to his feet and hurried to the other side of the room.

"What's it?"

"You reminded me of an old proverb I turned up in my research. 'The morning star alone knows where Kamehameha's bones are guarded.'" He dropped to his knees beside a large, diamond-shaped mark on the floor. "Another name for Venus is The Morning Star." He looked up at Isla, who was staring dumbfounded at him. "Got a knife?"

Isla shook her head.

"Here you go." Lark took out a large folding knife and slid it across the floor to him.

Maddock opened it and lined the point up with the center of Venus. If he was wrong, he might be the next victim of this strange room. Gritting his teeth, he raised the knife and plunged it downward. The glossy surface shattered, revealing a slot cut into the rock. Maddock inserted the knife into the slot and gave it a twist. It turned slowly and then locked into place.

Silence, and then a series of loud clacking sounds like giant boulders knocking together. The floor vibrated. In the center of the chamber, the section of floor on which the Naha Stone lay gradually flipped up onto its side.

"There's another part of the Naha Stone legend," Maddock said. "If someone were to overturn the stone, that person would be granted the power to unify all of Hawaii."

Isla nodded. "And the mana stored in the bones of Kamehameha the Great would be a prize for any aspiring ruler."

For a moment, things felt normal between them, two colleagues discussing a topic of mutual interest. It was over in an instant.

Where the stone had lain moments before was a round shaft. Stone steps were set in the wall, and they followed them down to the next level. Lark kept her eyes on Maddock and her hand close to her revolver. His success had not earned him any trust.

They found themselves standing before another pit, this one so deep they could not see the bottom. A stone bridge spanned the gap, leading to a pyramidal-shaped doorway on the opposite side. Five stone warriors stood single file in the middle of the bridge. They were clad only in seaweed. Their decaying flesh was sloughing off the bone. They were armed with spears and shark tooth clubs. The one in the lead held a conch shell to his lips.

"What are those?" Lark asked. For the first time, she appeared nervous.

"Nightmarchers," Maddock said. "They are the vanguard of a sacred king. They rise from the sea at night. They float above the ground, but witnesses report hearing their drums, conch shells, and the sound of marching feet."

"These statues are going to try to kill us, aren't they?" Lark asked.

Maddock looked the statues over. They were magnificent works of art, but they appeared purely ceremonial to him—a royal guard to escort the king on to the next world.

"I think we're safe from the statues, but the bridge might present a challenge." Its surface was set with hexagonal paving stones, each with a different image engraved on its surface—sea creatures and local flora and fauna. "I have a feeling there's a right way and a wrong way to do this."

"Does the legend mention a way to kill a Nightmarcher?" Lark asked.

"Pure light, whatever that means. And you can keep

them away by planting live shrubbery around your house."

"We want a shrubbery!" Isla said in a high-pitched voice.

Maddock didn't crack a smile. Their days of inside jokes were long past.

"Night-blooming jasmine. That's a shrub." Isla pointed to a distinctive pattern of leaves and blooms.

"You're sure about that?" Maddock asked.

"Pretty sure, but I'm still going to let you go first." Isla flashed a tentative smile, but it flickered and died.

"If it helps, night-blooming jasmine is known as the Queen of the Night," Lark offered. "A queen for the king."

"I'll take any connection I can get, however tenuous, at this point." Figuring there was no time like the present, Maddock stepped out onto the nearest jasmine tile. He held his breath as he put his full weight on it. Nothing exploded or otherwise ended his life and he saw no reason to stand around waiting for something bad to happen. He leaped from one stone to the next, keeping a sharp eye out for the so-called 'Queen of the Night'.

"You all right?" Isla called when he was halfway across.

"I'm not dead yet." He chimed instinctively, then kicked himself for the lapse. "Right now, I'm more concerned that one of these statues is going to fall on me. They are wobbly as hell."

To symbolize their ability to fly, the Nightmarchers had been set on blocks of quartz crystal. Now, the crystals were crumbling, and a couple of the statues were barely standing upright. Maddock figured that whatever trap or snare was lying outside the safe path, it wouldn't differentiate between a falling man and a falling statue. He slowed his pace and cautiously continued his trek across the void. When he came abreast of the last Nightmarcher, he paused.

"What in the hell?"

The first four Nightmarchers had been human—two

male, two female—the sculptor had rendered enough flesh on their decaying carcasses to make the distinction. But the last in line was something else entirely.

It had a narrow face, bulbous eyes, and a flat nose. The flesh that clung to its arms was scaly. Maddock was forcibly reminded of a discovery he and Bones had made on a recent expedition in South America. Another reptilian. But that was a mystery for another day.

He reached the other side safely and waited for Isla and Lark to catch up. A few paces away loomed the arched doorway into the next chamber. They shined their lights inside and Isla gasped.

"Oh, my Goddess! We found it!"

5

They were looking into a small chamber. Tiki masks hung from the walls. Sparkling mother-of-pearl covered the ceiling. The walls and floor were polished volcanic stone. And standing in the center was a sarcophagus of dark wood, its surface polished to a high sheen.

"I'd better go first, just to be safe," Maddock said.

"Be careful," Isla said.

Maddock made a thorough inspection of the chamber and saw no signs of hidden danger. Then he moved to the sarcophagus itself. No telling what might happen when he raised the lid. He took his time, circled it, looking it up and down. When he reached the far side, he paused, thinking.

"Everything all right?" Isla asked.

"The lid might be booby-trapped. Let me open it."

The truth was, he was reasonably satisfied that the tomb itself was not rigged with anything dangerous. He simply wanted to buy time to see if there were anything here he could turn to his advantage. But Isla was an impatient woman. She wouldn't wait long.

He took hold of the lid and lifted it. It was surprisingly light and came away easily. He propped it up on the opposite side of the sarcophagus, obscuring Isla's view. and looked inside.

Contrary to tradition, Kamehameha's flesh had not been stripped from his carcass and fed to the fishes. His full body had been laid to rest and it was perfectly preserved. He wore a gold sash, cape, and belt. A funeral mask covered his face.

Maddock frowned. As far as he was aware, such masks were not part of Hawaiian tradition, and he could tell immediately this mask was far too old to have been made for

Kamehameha. And then his eyebrows shot up. Not only was the mask itself out of place, but the face on the mask was not that of an ethnic Hawaiian, but of a European. The long, narrow nose with a rounded tip suggested Slavic ancestry. Maddock felt a spark of recognition but could not place the face.

Something else caught his eye, something very much out of place. Kamehameha clutched a stone cylinder. Maddock frowned. A Sumerian cylinder seal. Something so out of place it had to be important. He snatched it and tucked it inside his shirt.

"What's wrong?" Isla asked, a note of suspicion in her voice.

"Just giving it all a final check. It appears safe to me."

"We're coming in," Isla said.

Maddock moved aside.

Isla immediately spotted the death mask. Her eyes went wide, and she let out a tiny gasp. "This is it!" Isla said, leaning over the sarcophagus.

"Well, Maddock, you really did find it. I always thought Isla was winding me up with all those stories about her heroic ex," Lark said, eyeing him up and down. "Too bad you're not on our team."

"I'm not on any team," Maddock said. "I'm just another of your contractors."

Lark smiled sweetly. "That's exactly what you are. And you would do well to remember what happened to the others."

A bitter taste filled Maddock's mouth. Had Isla made a fool of him once again? Had she ever intended to let him go? And what about Spenser? In his pocket he still carried the folding knife Lark had lent him, but that was his only weapon.

"I want a closer look." Isla donned gloves and moved closer. Lark followed suit a moment later.

As they leaned down to remove the death mask, Maddock inched toward the door.

As she lifted the mask, Isla let out a cry of excitement while Lark let out a moan of intense satisfaction.

"The death mask of Ptolemy I," she breathed.

Now Maddock understood why the face on the mask looked familiar. Ptolemy I, or "Ptolemy Soter," was a Macedonian general and one of the closest companions of Alexander the Great. After Alexander's death, Ptolemy and his descendants ruled Egypt for three centuries until the death of the famed Cleopatra VII.

"You were right," Lark said. "Kamehameha did find his tomb!"

"But that is not what we are here for." Isla made a careful search of the king's clothing. Lark watched intently.

Maddock continued moving toward the door, a plan formulating in his mind, but he kept his eye on the two women.

"What do we have here?" Isla said. She reached into the sarcophagus and a few seconds later held up a leather thong. Suspended from it was a sphere of amber the size of a small egg.

Lark aimed her flashlight at it. When the beam struck it, she let out a gasp. At its center was a circle of bright gold, bisected by a vertical slash of obsidian.

"It looks like a snake's eye," Isla said, bemused. "I didn't expect that."

Even as he inched away, Maddock couldn't take his eyes off of the strange, gemlike sphere. Something about it was darkly hypnotic.

"I can't believe it," Lark said in a voice barely above a whisper. "We found the Eyes of Alexander!"

"One of them, anyway," Isla said, staring at the captivating eye. "Alexander's eyes, brown for the earth and blue for the sky." She said it in a voice barely above a whisper.

The women made a quick search of the body but found nothing else of interest.

"Arse!" Isla muttered. "I expected both of the eyes to be here."

"We possess one of the keys to Eden," Lark said. "That's all we need. Eden's treasure will be ours!"

The women suddenly looked at one another. Their entire demeanor changed. Something passed between them.

Maddock knew what was happening. Lark had let something slip that Maddock was not supposed to know, and now they were revisiting their promise to let him live. He didn't wait around to find out. He turned and ran.

"Lark, no!" Isla shouted.

The gunshot boomed like thunder in the narrow confines of the chamber. Pain lanced through his shoulder. Maddock gritted his teeth and kept running.

6

Drums pounded out a primordial beat. Spenser could not take her eyes off the approaching warrior. Torchlight gleamed in his dark eyes. Sweat glistened on his muscular frame. Suddenly, he let out a cry and thrust his spear in her direction. She let out a little yelp and leaned back too far in her chair. She overbalanced and fell backward. The warrior loomed over her for a split second, flashed a smile and a wink, and returned to the dance. Red-faced, she regained her feet and brushed the grass clippings off her shorts.

"I just had to wear white," she said, craning her neck to check for grass stains on her butt.

"Are you okay?" Her host Meri asked, setting Spenser's chair up for her.

"Only my pride injured. I got lost in the performance and he caught me by surprise."

"It happens more often than you might think. The music, the firelight, the mist rolling in off the ocean, it sucks you in." Meri gazed out across the open lawn, where the dancers performed for a small group of tourists who sat enjoying cocktails and watching the show.

"It's really something," Spenser said. "I will definitely include the dancers in my review."

"Review?" Meri blinked, then smiled. "Oh, yes! Your review of the resort. Sorry, my mind was elsewhere."

Spenser flashed a quick smile. Meri was an odd one. She was polite but constantly distracted. She was frequently checking her phone or looking around like she was expecting someone. Strange behavior for a host and guide.

"Is this an authentic performance? A traditional dance?" Spenser asked, taking out her pencil and notebook. She would ordinarily type her notes into an app on her smartphone, but she had turned it off to punish Maddock for ditching her.

Meri frowned. "I'm not sure." Again she checked her phone.

A pang of guilt ran through Spenser at the sight. What if Maddock had been trying to reach her? She had punished him long enough. She took out her phone and turned it on.

"Listen, if you need to make a call, it's no problem for me," Spenser said to Meri. "I'll be fine by myself for a few minutes."

"No, I'm to stay right by your side." The words came out in a rush. "Got to be a good host, you know."

Lights flashed and the fog machines belched out thick clouds of mist as the drumming rose to a crescendo. The dancers leaped and spun in choreographed combat.

As soon as Spenser's phone powered up, it pinged, notifying her that she had a message. She glanced at it. It was not from Maddock, but from his sister, Avery Halsey.

Get to a quiet place immediately. I have to talk to you.

Spenser pursed her lips. What could this be about?

It's an emergency.

Meri quirked an eyebrow. "Everything all right?"

"It's my mother," Spenser invented. Apparently, there's some sort of family emergency. Is there somewhere private I can go?"

"The restroom facilities are over there." Meri pointed to a freestanding hut a short distance away.

Spenser thanked her and made her way over to the small building. Instinct told her that something was very wrong. Maybe she'd spent too much time around Maddock and Bones, but her senses were suddenly on high alert. Meri's strange behavior, the odd text messages, and where the hell was Maddock? She had taken pity on him and excused him from the morning's activities, but he had been gone for hours.

"Probably down in some cave searching for the tomb Bones emailed him about," she muttered.

The restroom was unisex, with one door and no windows. An easy place to trap someone. She approached the door and then stole a glance back. Meri was looking at her phone again. Seizing the opportunity, Spenser made a beeline for a heavily landscaped island of palm trees, shrubs, and flowers. She melted into the foliage and stole a glance back. Meri was still looking at her phone. Heart racing, she tapped Avery's name on the screen.

Avery began talking as soon as she picked up. "Listen closely because time is of the essence. Where is my brother?"

"I don't know. He ditched me today. Probably looking for Kamehameha's Tomb. Good old Bones, ruining our vacation."

"It looks Maddock has once again gotten himself entangled with one of our targets, and he's dragged you along with him."

A lance of fear pierced Spenser's heart. Avery Halsey was part of a top-secret government intelligence team. If Maddock was mixed up with one of their targets, he could be in trouble. "Is he all right?"

"We were hoping he was with you. We've been trying to reach both of you."

Spenser's cheeks burned. Until this moment it hadn't occurred to her that Maddock could be in danger. Now her heart raced, and a cold fear settled in over her.

"Don't worry. Maddock always lands on his feet. Right now, I need to make sure you're safe. Has anyone around you been acting strange?"

"Yes. I've been assigned a host for the weekend and there's something not right about her. Matter of fact, she just made a comment about not leaving my side." No sooner had she uttered the words than Meri turned around and stared at the small hut a few meters away. "I think she suspects something," Spenser whispered.

"What is her name?" Avery asked sharply.

Meri, which is apparently short for Plumeria."

"Listen carefully. The job you are working is a sham. For reasons we did not know until now, some very dangerous people wanted Maddock to come to Lanai. Meri is one of them."

"Is this about the lost tomb Maddock's been going in about? If so, what do they want with me? He's the archaeologist."

"I don't know about a lost tomb, but I presume they want Maddock's expertise. As long as they have you, they can compel him to do what they want." She spoke in an unsettlingly matter-of-fact manner.

Spenser's mouth went dry. This was the sort of dangerous situation that Maddock and his crew encountered all the time in their treasure hunting endeavors, but she was new to it all, and it was terrifying.

"That's just great." She found sarcasm helped her remain calm.

"Help is on the way," Avery said. "We're tracking them on GPS, and they are minutes from you. You just need to stay safe until then."

"I will do my best," Spenser whispered. She lay facedown on the ground, flattening herself out to keep her profile below the level of the landscaping. "Are you sending some of your Argonauts, or whatever they're called?"

"Myrmidons, and no, our squad is very small, but we have…contacts vacationing on the big island. They are quite capable."

Just then, Meri stood and hurried over toward the hut. "The hourglass is almost out of sand," she muttered.

"Don't give up hope. The sand never leaves the hourglass. It just falls to the bottom."

"What the hell does that even mean?"

"Quiet. You're trying to avoid notice, remember?"

Spenser watched in silence as Meri entered the restroom and emerged a few seconds later, visibly angry. She waved toward the group of dancers who had just finished their performance. A trio of men, tall, muscular, and still carrying their primitive weapons, broke away from the group and trotted over to Meri. Their spearpoints flashed in the torchlight. Meri called Spenser's name, then took out her phone and tapped furiously.

In the quiet, the vibration of Spenser's phone sounded like a machine gun. Meri and her goons turned and headed in the direction of the sound.

"Shit!" Spenser silenced her phone, then began to crawl in the opposite direction. She reached the edge of the landscaped island and froze. It was about a fifty-meter sprint across open space to the resort's main building. No way she could make it.

"Are you okay?" Avery asked.

"No." Spenser quickly described her situation.

"I just need you to stay alive a little bit longer. The guys are literally seconds away from the hotel."

Spenser heard the roar of motorcycle engines in the distance, coming closer. Was that the sound of her rescuers? She stole a glance back. Meri and the warriors had fanned out and encircled her hiding place. Hiding was no longer going to cut it. It was time for action. She sprang to her feet and ran toward Meri, who was caught off guard by Spenser's attack.

Spenser punched Meri in the throat, gave her a shove that bowled her over, and made a beeline for the front parking lot. Running feet pounded on the soft grass behind her. She glanced back and saw the warriors were already closing in on her.

The roar of motorcycle engines rose to an ear-splitting whine. Up ahead, a pair of crotch rockets came flying over the berm that barred the way to the parking lot. They soared through the air, flew over Spenser's head, and landed between her and her pursuit.

One leather-clad rider laid the bike down on its side. The motorcycle skidded across the grass and slammed into the charging warriors, upending them like bowling pins. Bike and rider slid away across the soft earth, the rider stunned.

The second rider hopped off his bike in front of the warriors, who were slowly regaining their feet. One of them charged toward the biker, who ducked a wild haymaker and replied with a solid punch to the chin and a sidekick to the chest that sent him tumbling backward. The other two riders raised their fists, but before either could make a move, they were met with a barrage of punches from the biker.

Meri had avoided the bike and was charging toward Spenser. Spenser grabbed the closest weapon at hand—a tiki torch—and jammed it in the woman's face. Meri's hair caught fire. She let out a cry and began batting at the flames. Spenser swung the torch around like a baseball bat and clocked Meri across the side of the head. Fully routed, Meri and her soldiers turned and fled into the crowd that stood gawking at the bizarre scene.

"We hope you've enjoyed the show!" the biker boomed in a deep voice that seemed to fill the vast open space. It was a voice Spenser knew well. "That concludes this afternoon's performance."

He began to clap loudly. Spenser joined in. The second biker, still stuck underneath his motorcycle, paused in his struggles to join in the clapping. This was enough to convince the onlookers, who raised a smattering of polite applause for the odd performance, and quickly dispersed.

The rider pushed up his visor to reveal the face of a handsome Native American man. Bones Bonebrake was Maddock's business partner. The pair had been best friends since their days in the SEALs. He flashed a roguish grin.

"Before you yell at me, remember I just saved your ass."

"Bones! What the hell are you doing in Hawaii?"

"I'm with Grizzly." He inclined his in the direction of the second of her rescuers, who had finally gotten out from underneath his bike. "He hired me to help him do some location scouting."

Don "Grizzly" Grant was a television presenter specializing in adventure-themed programming. Spenser often worked with him on his projects. He was a loyal, if sometimes inept, friend.

"So, it's just a coincidence that you two are here when Maddock and I finally get some alone time?"

"Far as I know." Bones removed his helmet and looked around. "Speaking of Maddock, where is he?"

"Avery didn't tell you? He's been missing since this morning."

7

Maddock dashed along the bridge, trying to keep to the safe path and still avoid the bullets that zipped past his head and ricocheted off the statues that guarded the bridge. His shoulder burned from the wound he had already suffered. As he ran, every footfall made the Nightmarcher statues wobble on their precarious perches.

"I want him alive!" Isla shouted.

Maddock almost laughed. He had never heard of the Eyes of Alexander, nor any treasure associated with Eden, but it was obviously a secret they would kill to protect.

Just as he reached the far end of the line of stone sentinels, a lance of pain seared his calf. He had been hit again. He missed a step, his foot landed in the wrong place, and the stone beneath him crumbled. He threw his weight forward and landed on one of the stones engraved with the jasmine symbol. He felt a flash of relief. But his momentum kept him skidding forward. He twisted and fell awkwardly onto his side. His arm smashed through a wafer-thin layer of stone and he found himself looking down into abject blackness. He was still alive.

"That was too close."

"Hurry up! He's getting away!" Lark shouted

"This is not easy. Do you want to go first?" Isla said.

Maddock smiled. They were out on the bridge now. Perfect! He sprang to his feet, moved nimbly to the closest statue, and gave it a shove.

For once in his life, something worked on the first try. The heavy stone Nightmarcher tipped backward like a gullible younger sibling in a trust fall. It smashed into the second sentinel. Like giant dominos, the statues fell. As each one struck the bridge, tiles shattered. Lark let out an angry cry as a deep pit appeared directly in front of her.

"So clumsy of me!" Maddock shouted as he dashed for the stone stairs that led up into the Room of Snares. He took out the folding knife and searched the wall for his target. Voices echoed from down below.

"He can't have gotten far," Lark said.

Maddock grimaced. He had hoped the statue trick would buy him more time. But what he had in mind next ought to do the trick.

"Don't kill him," he heard Isla say. "We might need him again in the future."

"I think your obvious feelings for him are clouding your judgment," Lark said.

"Bollocks!" Isla said.

Maddock quickly found Paka'a, god of the wind He held his breath, then drove the butt of his knife into the god's oversized mouth. The rock crumbled and a thick cloud of gas poured out. Eyes burning, Maddock dashed out of the chamber and kept moving. Before long, heard Lark let out a frustrated shriek, followed by a retching cough.

"Can we get through it?" Lark wheezed.

"You are free to try," Isla said.

Maddock resisted the urge to smile. He had bought himself and Spenser some time, but neither of them was out of the woods yet.

When he reached the pit, Tama was standing guard. There was no way around the big man—only through him.

Maddock took Tama by surprise with his sudden charge. He plowed into the larger man, drove the crown of his head into Tama's chin. The blow wobbled Tama's knees, and the impact of their collision sent him tumbling to the ground. But he didn't stay down. He rose unsteadily to his feet, drew a machete, and backed toward the ladder—the only way out of the pit. Or was it?

Maddock made a show of drawing and opening his

purloined folding knife. He slowly circled to his right, knife extended.

"You're going to fight me with that little thing?" Tama barked a laugh and beckoned. "Come on. I dare you." He wobbled on his feet a little.

"You're dizzy," Maddock observed. "You should lie down."

"You hit hard for a little man," Tama admitted. "But I'm looking forward to snapping your neck."

The area beyond the desk was poorly lit. While Maddock melted into the shadows, Tama was content to remain in his position in front of the ladder.

"You can hide in the darkness all you want. The only way out is past me. He cracked his knuckles and laughed.

Maddock reached his destination—the cargo net attached to a rope and pulley that was used for moving heavy objects in and out of the pit. His hands found the safety rope that kept the counterweight suspended up above them. He grabbed hold of the rope and began cutting.

"Since you're going to kill me anyway, what is the Treasure of Eden?"

Tama let out a hiss. "Don't say that name. It is forbidden.

"Forbidden by whom?" Maddock said with a casual air as the knife sawed through the thick fibers.

"By the people who call the shots."

"What about the Eyes of Alexander?" Maddock's knife bit deeply into the rope. It began to fray.

"I thought you were supposed to be an expert." Tama paused. "Hold on. What are you doing?" He began to run toward Maddock.

"Come on! Come on!" Maddock sawed furiously at the last stubborn strands of rope.

With snapping and popping like firecrackers on the Fourth of July, the safety rope came free. Maddock grabbed hold of the cargo net with both hands and held on for dear life as it shot upward.

Tama made a leap for him. His fingertips brushed the heel of Maddock's boot as Maddock flew into the air. The big man cursed and shook his fist, then immediately let out a yelp and jumped back as the boulder that served as the counterweight crashed down in the exact spot where he had stood moments before

Maddock reached the top of the pit and clambered over the ledge. Down below, a flashlight flicked on. The beam slashed crazily through the darkness as Tama ascended the ladder. Maddock raced around the rim of the deep pit. Tama was halfway up when Maddock reached the top of the ladder. The beam of the light struck Maddock as he set his foot on the top rung.

"No!" Tama gasped. He hastily reversed course and scurried back down the ladder like a frightened crab.

Maddock kicked out and sent the ladder tipping over into space. Like a falling tree, it slowly crashed to the ground. Tama let out a shout of anger followed by a yelp of pain.

Maddock grinned. He hoped the man had broken something essential.

8

Maddock encountered no more resistance as he made his way out of the caves. As soon as he reached the jungle, he took out his smartphone, which his captors had not bothered to take from him. He understood the reason right away. No signal.

He realized this could work to his benefit. If he couldn't reach Spenser, that meant Isla could not get word to her people. Now it was a race. Maddock needed to get back to the hotel before Isla made it out of the caves. He took off at a dead run.

He rounded a bend and came face-to-face with Hunt, who was carrying a shovel. The man had two black eyes and he wore a bandage over his nose. Hunt's eyes went wide, and he froze in mid-step.

"You!" Hunt shouted.

The hesitation was all Maddock needed. Without breaking stride, he punched Hunt square on his broken nose. Hunt let out a wild cry of pain and dropped the shovel as he pressed his hands to his face. Maddock drove a side kick into Hunt's knee, buckling it and sending him falling to the ground. Before Hunt could recover, Maddock picked up the shovel and cracked him over the head. The big man fell flat on his face.

"Today is really not your day," Maddock said to the fallen man.

The old Bronco was still parked at the security gate. The keys were not in the ignition, but that was no problem. While Maddock lacked Bones' skills at hotwiring, this was the same make and model as the vehicle Maddock had driven for decades, and he knew it like the back of his hand.

Minutes later, he was flying back down the dirt road.

When he finally reached a paved road there were no road signs to point the way. He chose the downhill route. His phone began to vibrate as notifications popped up. Numerous texts and missed calls from Spenser, Bones, and Avery.

He tapped on Spenser's name. She picked up on the first ring.

"Are you safe?" she asked without preamble.

"Yes. And you?"

"I am now. Bones and Grizzly are on speakerphone. Avery sent them"

"Wait a minute. What are they doing here?"

"They just *happened* to be in the islands at the same time we were."

"We're scouting locations for my next program," Grizzly piped up.

"What's the project?" Maddock asked.

"An investor wants me to develop a series centered around the search for Kamehameha's Tomb."

Maddock cursed. He should have known Isla was pulling Grizzly's strings. She had been working with Grizzly when she and Maddock first met.

"I think your investor is the same person who abducted me. I have a hunch your project has been canceled."

"Where are you?" Spenser asked.

"I don't actually know. Hold on a minute." Using his smartphone to check his location and found that he was still on Lanai. "I'm on the southeast part of the island. Just a couple of miles from the resort."

"Meet us at the airport," Bones said. "We're getting out of here."

"Will do." Maddock hung up the phone and was about to step on the gas when flashing blue lights appeared in the rearview mirror. He moved to the side to make way, but the officers pulled in behind them.

He brought the Bronco to a stop. Behind him, the officers sprang from their patrol car and approached with sidearms drawn. He put his hands in the air and called back to them.

"I know I was driving too fast but there's no need for weapons," he said.

"Get out of the car and lie face down, sir."

What was going on here? Were these men in on whatever conspiracy Isla was cooking up? They didn't look like impostors.

"Sir, get out of the car now!" the officer shouted.

"Can you at least tell me what I did wrong?" Maddock asked.

"The car you're driving was stolen three days ago."

Maddock closed his eyes and let out a groan. He had stolen a stolen car. Even when she wasn't trying, Isla had a knack for ruining his day.

9

"**We're not going** to make it in time," Lark said.

"Lark, if you say that one more time, I swear to the Goddess," Isla said. Lark had done nothing but complain since they had emerged from the tomb only to discover Maddock had stolen their car.

They trudged along in silence, Hunt and Tama hacked a path for them with their machetes. The peace and quiet lasted only a few minutes.

"You know something?" Lark said. "I used to laugh at the way your face glows whenever you talk about Maddock. Now that I've seen him in action, I understand. He's competent; that's a rare trait in a man."

"I do not glow." Isla's ears burned and she turned her head away.

"What happened between you two if you don't mind my asking?"

"I do mind," Isla snapped. She took a deep, calming breath. It was wrong to be at odds with a sister over a man. "It was my choice. I had to do what was best for all concerned."

"He's available then?" Lark asked. "I mean, once the girlfriend is disposed of."

"You just tried to kill him," Isla said.

"That was business. It would be simpler if he were dead. Now that he's free, we have to assume he's already reported everything to the authorities. Cow's out of the barn."

"Agreed." Isla hoped the others couldn't see the relief flooding through her. She had never wanted Maddock dead. Her desire to keep him alive was the reason she had betrayed his trust in the first place. But she could never make him understand that.

"We've found what we came for. Let the university have the place."

The jungle was thinning out. Up ahead the glint of sunlight on water caught her eye.

"Nearly there," Tama said. "I can see the ocean."

"Any word from Meri?" Lark asked.

Isla took out her smartphone. "Still no service. But she knows the protocol."

"Assume it's all gone tits-up, let the girl go, and make a dash for the escape pod."

"I don't care for that idiom," Isla said.

Lark tilted her head, frowned. "Escape pod?"

Isla closed her eyes." Never mind.

A boat was anchored off the coast as arranged. Isla signaled and soon a small craft was cutting through the waters in their direction. They were surprised to see Meri at the helm. She helped them aboard, not meeting Isla's eye. When they were headed out to the fishing boat, it all came spilling out.

"It was a disaster," Meri said. "Someone tipped off the girl and she tried to sneak away. Just as I was catching up with her a couple of dudes on motorbikes showed up. Your hired goons made a run for it."

"What did *you* do?" Lark asked, a note of mockery in her voice.

"What do you think I did? I got the hell out of there, disposed of the surplus labor, and came directly here. I even traveled on foot so there would be no abandoned vehicle to point the authorities in our direction. Is that enough for you?"

"Shut up, both of you," Isla said.

"Thank you," Hunt said under his breath.

"That goes for everyone." Isla rested her head in her hands. "Did you see who rescued Spenser?"

"I caught a glimpse of one of them. He was a big dude, a native but not an islander."

"Bonebrake," Isla muttered. "He's Maddock's best mate. How did he know?"

"Am I to be punished?" Meri asked.

Isla shook her head. "It's probably for the best. They can go on with their lives and we can continue on our mission."

Meri's eyes went wide. "You mean you found it?"

Isla took out the Eye of Alexander and held it up for all to see.

"That's the brown one. Where's the blue one?" Meri asked.

"It wasn't with Kamehameha, which means it was not buried with Ptolemy. If only we had the entire book instead of fragments."

"But we only need one to get in, right?" Meri asked.

"That is what the legends say, but I'd prefer to have both."

"A key to Eden," Lark moaned as if she were in the throes of religious ecstasy. "One step closer to destiny."

10

Maddock sat in the corner of the small jail cell, eyes half-closed. Two men sat on the other side of the cell, both of them very large and very drunk. Their heads were close together as they tried and failed to keep their voices down.

"Look at him pretending to be calm," one of them said. "Bet you he's scared to death."

"Stupid tourist," the other man said. "Let's give him an island welcome."

Maddock groaned internally. This day just kept getting better and better. No point in wasting time. He stood, cracked his knuckles.

"He thinks he's tough," the first man said. The big fellow clenched his fists and stood.

Maddock didn't wait around for any more of their weak attempts at intimidation. He poured all his anger and frustration into a right cross that shattered the man's front teeth. He spun and drove a front kick into the other man's unprotected groin. The fellow made a squelching sound and sank to the floor.

"What is your problem?" the first man said through a mouthful of blood. He backed away, fingers pressed to his lips.

Somewhere out of sight, a door squealed open on rusty hinges and footsteps resounded on the concrete floor.

"What's going on in there?" a voice barked.

"These two drunks are fighting," Maddock said. "Can you put me in a private cell? I'd like to take a nap."

An officer appeared at the cell door. He ignored the protests of the two intoxicated men.

"No need. You're being transferred into federal custody."

"What are you talking about?" Maddock demanded.

He had his answer an instant later when an attractive woman with short black hair and dark brown skin stepped up to the cell door.

"Lord Jesus, what happened in here?" Tam Broderick said. "Actually, I don't want to know. Come on, Maddock."

"Don't you want to cuff him?" the officer asked.

"He won't give me any trouble, will you?" Tam asked. Maddock shrugged. "That's good enough for me. Come on."

Maddock's smartphone was returned to him, but not the cylinder from Kamehameha's tomb. He glanced at Tam.

"I've taken possession of the artifact." There was a twinkle in her eye that foretold some horse-trading in his immediate future.

"Thanks for bailing me out, and for the help with Spenser," he said as they stepped out into the hot afternoon sun.

"You're welcome." She didn't need to remind him he was once again deep in her debt. They had known each other too long for that.

They hopped into a white Escalade with leather seats.

"Nice ride," Maddock said. "The government lets you rent something this fancy?"

"The government barely knows I exist anymore." Her voice was bitter.

"Things quiet with the Dominion?" The Dominion was an extremist movement that had infiltrated governments around the world. At a grassroots level, they sought power by radicalizing religious zealots.

"Haven't you been paying attention? The Dominion is mainstream now. They don't call themselves that, of course. They're getting elected to office, being appointed to the bench. Their talking heads are now mainstream celebrities."

Maddock nodded. He had made similar observations of late.

"How did it all go so bad so fast, Maddock?"

"There's more power in confirming what people already believe than there is in making them face hard truths."

"Amen," Tam said.

"How full is your swearing jar?"

"Cussing jar," she corrected. "I filled it up, gave it to my auntie for Christmas. She took a trip to Vegas and had money left over."

Maddock laughed. After all these years he still couldn't decide how he felt about Tam. He respected her, even enjoyed her company at times, but she was far too secretive for his liking.

"About the cylinder. You know it would be illegal for me to let you have it."

Maddock wanted to swear but wasn't sure if he'd be required to contribute to her cussing jar. He swallowed hard and forced a smile. "I figured." He supposed he couldn't be too angry. She had, after all, saved the day. "Consider it a gift in appreciation of services rendered."

"You writing Hallmark cards?"

Maddock grinned.

"Before you ask," Tam said abruptly. "I wasn't monitoring your communications. I've been keeping an eye on Isla Mulheron."

Maddock gritted his teeth. He still couldn't believe Isla had abducted him.

"She made a fool of me yet again. What are the Tuatha up to, anyway?"

"The Tuatha appear to have formed an alliance with our old friends, the Sisterhood. I think the Sisterhood is ultimately pulling the strings."

This time Maddock did curse. Tam waved it away.

"That one's on the house. You've had a long day."

"I suppose it makes sense. The Tuatha and the

Sisterhood are built on common ground: paganism, nationalism, and mysticism."

"The climate is ripe for that sort of thing. I still can't believe Don Krueger left witness protection and now has his own radio show." Krueger was an expert in legends and conspiracies who had run afoul of powerful people who would prefer certain secrets not see the light of day. "He doesn't feel he's in danger now. With all the craziness in the world, he's just one more voice in the wind."

"Now that's a Hallmark card," Maddock said.

"A cynical one. Now tell me what happened today. Please," she added.

Maddock quickly recounted the day's events, from his abduction, to the discovery of the tomb, and his escape.

"Eyes of Alexander?" Tam said. "You heard of them?"

Maddock shook his head. Nor have I heard of keys to Eden or a treasure."

"Isla is also a suspect in the theft of a private collection of scroll fragments reputed to have come from the Library of Alexandria. No idea what was written on them."

"So, the Sisterhood is looking for a treasure associated with Eden." Maddock chuckled.

"Why is that funny?"

"If you believe in a worldwide flood, then the land of Eden is no more. The antediluvian world was destroyed."

Tam shrugged. "If the Sisterhood is looking for something, I want to know what it is. Even if I'm not permitted to take direct action anymore." Maddock had never seen Tam in such a dark mood.

"You mention the Great Library of Alexandria. Is there any mention of Eden among the documents we found a few years back?" During the search for Atlantis, they had discovered a veritable treasure trove of ancient world documents and artifacts beneath one of Washington D.C.'s most famous monuments. The contents included scrolls believed to have come from the Great Library.

"We didn't get half of it inventoried before we were shut down by the powers-that-be. I don't know what became of it."

"That's disappointing. Any idea how Kamehameha fits in?" Maddock asked.

"All we know is a short while after the thefts, Isla popped up at the head of a university-sponsored dig here on the island. I wish I knew more, but until now, I couldn't justify allotting any more of my limited resources to surveilling her."

"Why now?"

Tam smirked. "She involved you. You are what I like to call the first domino. I try to keep you from falling." She paused, smiled coyly. "Unless I'm the one tipping you over."

"You said it, not me." Maddock grinned. "I really am trying to keep out of trouble, but it seems to follow me."

"You sound like Bonebrake."

"Yeah, but in my case it's true."

Tam smiled, but quickly grew serious.

"I'm in a difficult situation, Maddock. We've got billionaires and corporate interests trying to become the American version of Russian oligarchs, and judges and politicians scrambling to sell their souls to them. I can move freely to a certain degree, but I'm very limited in what I can do outside our borders beyond research and surveillance."

"And you have never colored outside the lines," Maddock joked.

"I can't do it like I used to. We mostly gather intel and pass it up the chains these days. We keep our ears to the ground for stirrings among the usual suspects, but major operations have to be approved from above."

"That has to be difficult."

"Especially when you don't know which of your superiors are legit and which ones have been bought and paid for. I mostly keep within my budget and try to do as much as I'm sure I can get away with."

As they approached the entrance to the airport, Tam reached into her handbag, took out the seal, and handed it to him.

"You're giving this to me?" Maddock asked.

"We both know you aren't going to let this go. I'm convinced this is important, but I can't take a direct hand in the investigation. Might as well let someone I trust handle it."

"What's the catch?"

Tam laughed and shook her head. "Lord Jesus, why did you curse me with this man?" she said to the sky. "Just keep me in the loop. Maybe I can find a way to help."

"Deal."

She brought the Escalade to a stop alongside the tiny airport terminal.

"Now get the hell out of my car. Your friends are waiting for you."

Maddock looked out across the tarmac to see Spenser, Bones, and Grizzly waiting by a small plane. Spenser and Grizzly waved happily. Bones grinned and gave him the finger.

Tam and Maddock shook hands and each wished the other good luck. As Tam sped away, Maddock couldn't help but wonder if everything was as it seemed.

11

Maddock was still puzzling over his conversation with Tam when Spenser grabbed him by the collar, hauled his head down, and planted a firm kiss on his lips. Then she took a step back and looked him up and down like a horse trader examining a prize stallion.

More like a broken-down mule in my case, he thought.

"Are you all right?" Spenser asked.

"A few bruises. The usual."

"What's up with that bandage around your calf?" Bones asked. "And what's up with your shoulder?"

Maddock gritted his teeth. Leave it to Bones to point that out.

"It was only a couple of grazes."

"You got shot?" Spenser put her hands to her mouth.

"Purely superficial. I promise." He reached out to take her hand, but she turned and stalked away, boarding the plane in a huff."

"Thanks for that, Bones. I really appreciate it."

"Any time," Bones said.

Grizzly, an emotional man, gave Maddock a much longer hug than necessary. Maddock clapped him on the back and extricated himself from the embrace as quickly as courtesy would allow.

"Thanks for rescuing Spenser," Maddock said to Grizzly.

"You should have seen it, Maddock! I put my bike into a skid and took those guys down. After that, they turned tail and ran. I would have caught them, too, but I got stuck under my bike."

"Glad you're okay." Maddock grinned and flicked a glance at Bones, who mouthed, *He crashed.*

The pilot was named Phyllis. She was a stocky woman with a buzz cut and a clipped manner. She ran through her preflight instructions quickly, in the manner of a teacher conducting a review session.

"Buckle up, and we'll be on our way." Phyllis barked the order like a good drill sergeant.

"Did you serve?" Bones asked as they taxied down the runway.

"Damn right I did." She didn't elaborate.

The conversation quickly turned to Maddock's abduction and what he had discovered in the maze of volcanic passageways.

"...and then I stole the Bronco and called you guys, not knowing that I was driving a car that had already been reported stolen."

"Criminals stealing a car. Imagine that!" Spenser said in mock amazement. The others laughed.

"Do you know your abductors' identities?" Bones asked.

Maddock cleared his throat. "Well, the girl who drugged me is named Lark. She's also the one who shot me."

"Want me to add her to our Christmas card list?" Spenser asked blandly.

"And the two goons were named Tama and Hunt."

"How about the boss lady?" Grizzly asked.

"It was Isla Mulheron," he said.

Bones and Grizzly began to spew curses. Spenser shouted and gesticulated. Each had their own reasons to dislike the woman. Maddock had a sinking feeling their rants could go on for some time.

"Settle down back there!" Phyllis snapped over the intercom.

The effect was immediate. Their voices dropped to a whisper.

"I promise you, I was not happy to see her," Maddock

said.

"This is going to make for a great social media video," Spenser said. "And I've already got a title for it." She held up her hands as if beholding a marquee. "*I Got Abducted by My Boyfriend's Ex! How's Your Day Going?*"

"I would watch that," Bones said.

"Everybody would watch it. But of course, I can't make that video because it would interfere with you guys saving the world and all that." She stuck out her lower lip, then smiled. "It's okay, Maddock. I know you live a different kind of life, but I *will* give you a hard time about it every now and then."

"Fair enough."

"So, what's the Treasure of Eden?" Grizzly asked. "Because it sounds like an amazing documentary. Maybe even a television series."

"I already have so many marketing ideas!" Spenser said.

Bones and Maddock looked at one another and shook their heads as the pair began to brainstorm a marketing plan.

"Maybe we should discuss the content of the show before we start selling a product that doesn't exist," Bones said.

"Fine. Let's start with the Garden of Eden story. I know about the fig leaves and the part about blaming the woman for everything," Spenser said.

"According to Abrahamic religions, it was paradise. God planted a garden eastward in the land of Eden, near a place where two cherubim with flaming swords guarded the Tree of Life. In that garden, God created Adam and Eve."

"Just Adam and Eve? Nobody else?" Spenser asked. "How does that work genetically without a viable breeding population?"

"The scriptures say Adam and Eve's children married the 'children of men.'"

"Where did they come from?" Spenser asked.

"I don't know. And can we hold the questions until the end of the lecture?"

"No promises." Spenser crossed her arms and sat back in her seat.

"Maybe God created a bunch of people," Bones said. "But the rest weren't worth mentioning because they weren't the first. It's like the *Guinness Book of World Records*. Nobody cares who ate the second-most hot dogs."

"Adam and Eve lived in the garden with God," Maddock continued, "and everything was perfect. They were safe and cared for. The only rule they had to follow was that they could not eat the fruit from the Tree of the Knowledge of Good and Evil."

"That's a mouthful." Grizzly turned to Spenser. "We'll need to come up with a different name for the tree. Maybe a fruit-related sponsor?"

"Way ahead of you." Spenser's nails clicked lightly against the smartphone screen as she took notes.

Maddock figured he should keep going and allow them to interrupt as needed.

"In the end, the serpent persuaded Eve to tempt Adam into tasting the fruit. When God returned to the garden, they hid from him because for the first time they were ashamed of their naked bodies. When God confronted them, Adam said, *'The woman* you *made for me* made me *do it.'*"

Spenser and Grizzly both snorted and tossed their heads.

"You knew that part was coming," Maddock said. "Anyway, they were driven from the garden and made to live in our world. Adam's punishment was a life of hard labor. Eve's punishment was the pain of childbirth."

Spenser frowned, scratched her head. "So, it's just a cautionary tale to warn kids not to have sex."

"What are you talking about?" Bones ask.

"The garden is our childhood home where our parents

take care of us. We're safe and secure, but we aren't in charge of our own lives. Tasting the fruit is what happens when a woman spends too much time around the serpent."

"Hold on, you're saying the serpent represents..."

"Obviously. You think the storyteller chose the word serpent by accident? They were practically drawing you a picture."

Maddock frowned, scratched his chin. He was so deeply immersed in the traditional story that he had never considered from such a different perspective.

"The fruit could also symbolize reproduction," Maddock said.

"And once you start tasting the fruit, that's when you leave home and make your own way in life," Grizzly said.

"And the best part is, none of it is the guy's fault," Spenser said. "The woman and his serpent made him do it."

Maddock nodded. It made sense. The first part of the book of Genesis described the creation of the universe, the second the creation of the earth and all of its living creatures. Seen from a certain perspective, the Garden of Eden story could be understood as the act of creation on earth being passed along to the human race.

"What about Lilith?" Grizzly asked. "My girlfriend and her feminist friends practically worship her."

"She's not part of Biblical canon," Maddock said.

"Coverup," Bones fake-coughed into his hand.

"Fine. You explain it," Maddock said.

"Depending on the tradition, she's either a succubus or Adam's ex-wife," Bones said. "Pretty much the same thing, if you think about it."

"Well, maybe if Adam didn't let the serpent do his thinking for him." Grizzly raised his hand and Spenser gave him a no-look high-five.

"If we set the metaphor aside and presume that there was an actual place that inspired the Eden legend, where would we look?" Spenser asked.

"That depends on which version of the story you read," Maddock said. "But even if you take into account similar stories from other cultures in the region, there still aren't very many clues. The Bible places it at the headwaters of four rivers. It's generally assumed that the Tigris and Euphrates in the Middle East are two of those rivers. But there are legends that place the Garden in spots all over the world."

"Do you have a favorite theory?" Grizzly asked.

"Beneath the Persian Gulf, in a place that wasn't underwater thousands of years ago," Maddock said. It was a pet theory he had been working on for some time.

"There are better theories," Bones said. "And by better, I mean theories that aren't boring." He raised a big finger. "Eden exists on earth, but on a different spiritual plane. Maybe the key Maddock saw could somehow take you there."

"That's too sci-fi," Grizzly said. "I can't sell that."

"Second theory," Bones said loudly, "is that Eden is another name for the land beneath the Earth. I like that one better."

"But how does Kamehameha fit in?" Maddock said. "And what's the significance of this thing?" He held up the cylinder seal he had taken from the tomb.

"After we got your call, I lined up someone on the Big Island who might be able to help us," Bones said. "She's an expert in the field."

"How did you manage that on such short notice?" Spenser asked.

Bones glanced away. "It's somebody Maddock and I know. We go back a long way."

"Who is it?" Grizzly asked.

Bones shifted uncomfortably in his seat. "You know, maybe Isla showing up was an omen."

Maddock sat up in his seat so hard that his seatbelt felt

like it would cut him in half. "You called Jade? Are you kidding me?"

Jade Ihara was an archaeologist, an academic, and another of Maddock's exes. Their relationship was not exactly icy, but there was little warmth there.

Spenser caught on a moment later. "Jade Ihara? Oh, my God!" She looked around. "Is this a video game? Am I Scott Pilgrim?"

Maddock didn't get the reference but he guessed the comparison was not a positive one. Spenser had grabbed her backpack and was rifling through it.

"You don't have a weapon in there, do you?" he asked.

"I do, but that's not what I'm looking for right now." She pulled out a compact and checked her face in the mirror. "If I have to meet Lara Croft's hotter sister, I'm doing it with good makeup."

Laughing, Maddock turned and looked out the window at the late afternoon sun. Its orange rays glinted off the starboard wing.

Starboard?

"What's with you, Maddock?" Bones asked. "You look like you just watched Nancy Pelosi make a sex tape with Mitch McConnell."

"Something just occurred to me. If we are flying south to the Big Island, shouldn't the sun be on the port side of the craft?"

"You're right," Bones said. "Grizzly, what airline did you use?"

"Airline?" Grizzly scratched his head. "No, this plane belongs to the outfit that hired me." He paused, gaped. "That means..." He couldn't finish the sentence.

Maddock unbuckled his seatbelt and rose to his feet. "That means it belongs to the Sisterhood,"

As if in confirmation, the cockpit door swung open. He caught a glimpse of Phyllis, who tossed something into the cabin. Maddock knew what it was before fog began pouring out of it.

"Gas grenade!"

12

Maddock made a dash for the cabin door and grabbed it just before Phyllis could slam it shut. As they struggled, they began to feel the effects of the gas. Although he held his breath, his sinuses burned, and his eyes began to water.

Phyllis released the door without warning and Maddock stumbled back and tripped over someone lying on the floor. It was Bones.

"You stepped on my hand," Bones said. His eyes were already glazed from the effects of the gas.

Maddock regained his feet and ran for the cockpit. A rush of air met him. Through the thinning cloud of gas from the grenade, he could see Phyllis cranking open the flight deck side window. She wore a parachute strapped to her back.

As she tried to escape, Maddock grabbed the husky woman by the belt and hauled her back.

"Not so fast," he said.

Phyllis kicked back, driving her heel into Maddock's gut. He let out a grunt and lost his grip. It was all the time Phyllis needed. She forced her bulk through the window and was away.

Through the open window, Maddock saw her give him the finger before her parachute opened. Someone behind him coughed and Maddock turned to see Bones peering into the cabin.

"She got away," Maddock said.

"Right now, I'm more concerned with who is flying the plane."

The words hit Maddock like a punch. How could he have been so stupid? He glanced at the pilot's seat. The plane was on an even keel at the moment but losing altitude.

"I can't believe you never got your pilot's license," Bones said.

"Neither did you."

Just then, Grizzly shoved past Bones and settled into the chair. His eyes and nose were streaming from the effects of the gas.

"I can fly," he said. "Done it loads of times." He began flipping switches with practiced ease.

"Are we sure about this?" Spenser called from the cabin.

"He looks like he knows what he's doing," Bones said. "Maddock's going to take the copilot's seat just in case."

"That's not comforting," Spenser said.

"Thanks for that." Maddock took his seat and watched the water beneath them getting closer and closer. They were closing in on the island of Oahu.

"We're losing altitude," he said.

"I know. I'm just working out how to turn this thing around." Grizzly said.

"You mean you don't know?" Maddock's heart raced.

"I've got it narrowed down. I think this is it."

The next thing Maddock knew, they were plunging downward at a steep angle. They were closing in on a harbor where a familiar monument shone in the sunlight. He recognized it immediately.

"Grizzly, do you know what that is down there?"

"Do me a favor, Maddock. Give me the grand tour after I've gotten the plane under control.

Maddock almost laughed. It was the first time the gregarious television presenter had ever snapped at him.

They closed in on the harbor, close enough now that Maddock could see tourists gawking and pointing. A few broke and ran as the small plane closed in on them.

"Pull up! Pull up!" Maddock barked.

"I'm trying." The plane rolled left, then banked sharply

to the right.

"So, that's what that does," Grizzly said.

"Are you kidding me? You said you could fly."

"We're still in the air, aren't we?" Grizzly said.

Still losing altitude, he brought the plane about and headed back toward the harbor. They soared over a football stadium, passing inches above the press box.

"Yo, Maddock," Bones shouted. "I think I just found religion!"

"Grizzly, we need altitude." Years in the service had drilled into him the ability to remain calm in even the most extreme situations.

"I've got a plan. See that thing?" Grizzly pointed to a long, white structure that ran out onto the water. Its concave roof shone like a diamond against the cobalt waters.

"The *USS Arizona Memorial*?" Maddock didn't like where this was headed.

"I'm going to do a touch-and-go landing. We'll springboard right back up into the air."

Maddock's mouth was dry. Slowly he turned to look at the television personality.

"What flight training do you have, exactly?"

"Oh, I'm a licensed pilot. Well, I was a licensed pilot, but I haven't kept my credentials current. But I've kept sharp playing video games. *Baron of Blood* is awesome. It's an old World War I, first-person shooter game."

The stark, white memorial filled their field of vision. Tourists screamed and ran..

"Grizzly, are the landing gear even down?" Maddock shouted.

"Oh, good point. Change of plans." Grizzly turned the control wheel and the airplane banked sharply. They missed the memorial by inches.

Maddock closed his eyes, took a few calming breaths, and resisted the urge to strangle his friend. He waited a full ten seconds before he spoke.

"Why didn't you do that in the first place?" he said through gritted teeth.

"I really wanted to do the touch-and-go. It would have been epic."

"I have to agree with him," Bones shouted.

"Would have made a great video," Spenser chimed in.

"Nobody asked either of you," Maddock said.

"Sorry, Dad," Bones said.

"You've got it under control?" he asked Grizzly.

"Absolutely." Grizzly's wavy, brown hair bounced as he nodded enthusiastically. "You know what the best part of it is?"

"There's a best part?" Spenser said.

"If anybody identifies our plane, Isla's outfit will be blamed for it."

13

Isla Mulheron sat in a coffee shop sipping black tea and waiting for a phone call. She looked around nervously at the tourists who hurried past. A man glanced in her direction, eyed her up and down. She glared back and his lascivious grin melted under the heat of her gaze.

"You look troubled," Lark said.

"I don't like it when people stray from the plan."

When Maddock and his friends landed in their laps, Phyllis had taken the initiative to bring them to Isla. Now she was faced with the difficult decision of how to deal with them. Maddock and Bones were valuable resources, but difficult to control at the best of times. Being abducted for the second time that day would only make Maddock more obstinate. She doubted she could secure their aid without compelling them in some way. But could she let them go and still maintain the respect and loyalty of her team? She didn't have much time to decide. Last she had heard, the plane was on its way to a secure location.

"Phyllis saw an opportunity and seized it." Lark took a sip of her macchiato. How she could stand the sweet drink Isla had no idea. "Isn't that what you want from your team?"

"We've gotten what we need out of him. Phyllis has only complicated things."

"You could hand them over to Hunt and Tama. They have a list of creative things they plan on doing to Maddock when they get their hands on him again." Lark took another sip of her drink and pursed her lips thoughtfully. "I hope they don't mess up his face. He's quite handsome."

Isla shook her head. Sometimes Lark behaved like a schoolgirl—in love one minute, ready to kill someone the next. Day by day her team was getting harder to manage.

"Sorry. I forgot you still have feelings for him."

"No, I don't," Isla said, much too quickly. She had all sorts of feelings where Maddock was concerned, but it didn't matter. She could never make him understand.

Lark made a face and let the subject drop. "Can I look at the eye again?"

"Not out here in the open."

"Oh, come on. No one knows what it is. To the uninitiated, it just looks like a piece of costume jewelry."

Reluctantly, Isla reached inside her blouse and pulled out the eye, which she wore around her neck.

"So shiny!" Lark cupped the gem. "I feel different when I touch it."

"How so?" Isla hadn't felt a thing when she slipped it on.

"It's hard to explain. It's like it's trying to talk to me, and I almost understand the language."

"Let me know if it starts speaking English. Maybe it could point us to a doorway."

"A doorway to Eden," Lark breathed. She lapsed into silence, gazed at the orb. "What do you think she's like?" she said abruptly.

"Who?" Isla asked absently. A small plane, flying low, was zipping toward the harbor.

"Lilith. What will it be like to stand in her presence?" Lark's voice was a mere whisper, but it startled Isla.

"You shouldn't talk about that in public."

"No one is listening," Lark rolled her eyes. "And if they were, they wouldn't know what we're talking about."

Lilith, according to extra-Biblical sources, was Adam's first wife, created from the earth at the same time as Adam. As the scripture read, *"In the image of God He created them; male and female he created them."* Being equals, Adam and Lilith would not concede to one another. Lilith eventually left, and God was forced to make a new mate for Adam. Eve was a lesser creation, made from Adam's rib rather than from the Earth itself. Where Lilith was Adam's equal, Eve was expected to take a subservient role. Over time, Lilith was literally demonized. Many accounts described her as an evil spirit, inhuman.

"Even if Lilith was an actual person who once lived, that was thousands of years ago," she whispered.

Lark shrugged, then her eyes went wide, and she sprang up from her chair and pointed out over the water. "Is that our plane?"

The whine of the small engine grew louder as the airplane Isla had spotted moments earlier swept down over the harbor, headed directly for the *USS Arizona* memorial. People stopped what they were doing to stare. Screams rang out around the memorial, tourists scattered and ran.

"What is Phyllis doing?" Lark asked.

Invisible hands wrapped around Isla's throat as she watched the mad descent. What was happening? And then she understood. A flood of certainty swept over her, and she found her voice again.

"I don't think that's Phyllis' doing. I think it's Maddock."

The plane buzzed the shining white monument, missing it by inches. It banked sharply, then turned south, heading out across the harbor and toward the ocean.

"Damn you, Phyllis," she muttered. She drained her tea and turned to Lark. "We're going to have to move much faster now."

"Why is that?" Lark asked.

"Two reasons. First of all, that plane could be traced back to us, which makes it essential that we get beyond the reach of American intelligence as quickly as possible."

"American intelligence." Lark smirked. "Isn't that an oxymoron?"

"Sometimes. But don't underestimate them all. Some

are quite capable." She stared at the plane as it shrank to a white dot on the horizon.

"You said there were two reasons," Lark prompted.

"There are. Thanks to Phyllis, now there is no way Maddock will give up the hunt until he has found Eden."

14

Don Ho College was a small, picturesque campus on the island of Maui. The neatly landscaped grounds were thick with palms, lush grass, and bougainvillea in full bloom. They quickly found the Natural History Building and located Jade's office.

"Doctor Jade Ihara, Professor of Archaeology," Bones read aloud. "Can you imagine having her as a professor? Get an answer wrong and she'd probably…"

Before Bones could finish the sentence, the door swung open to reveal an attractive woman with brown eyes, lustrous black hair, and no discernible smile lines.

"Hello, Bones," Jade said flatly.

"Hey, Jade," Bones said, unabashed. "Thanks for helping us out on short notice."

Maddock thought that might be the most civil exchange he had ever seen between the pair. The two had been allies at times, but never friends.

"What happened to you?" Bones pointed to Jade's left foot, which was in a walking boot.

"Climbing," she said in a tone that indicated that was all she had to say on the matter.

"Climbing or falling?" Bones quirked an eyebrow.

"Screw you, Bones." Jade glanced past Bones and her eyes flared. "You didn't tell me you were bringing *him* along."

Here we go, Maddock thought. For all her good qualities, Jade could hold a grudge like no other. "I didn't have anything to do with this," he began.

Jade turned toward him, an expression of surprise on her face.

"Oh, Maddock. Sorry, I didn't notice you. This your

girlfriend?" She reached out and shook Spenser's hand. "I'm Jade."

"Spenser, nice to meet you." Spenser appeared to be almost disappointed in Jade's bland reaction. Doubtless, she had been working herself up for some sort of confrontation, or at least an exchange of thinly veiled jibes.

"Sorry if I'm abrupt," Jade said. "I just didn't expect that moron to show up at my door." She jabbed a finger in Grizzly's direction. "He's been trying for years to get me to work on his idiotic ancient mystery shows. I'm a scientist, not a bimbo."

Spencer turned a delicate shade of pink and cleared her throat. Maddock gave a quick shake of his head. She made a face at him but kept her silence.

"Grant, I don't appreciate you using these assclowns to try and rope me in," Jade turned toward Grizzly and raised her voice. "And I really don't like you showing up where I work."

"Who's an assclown?" Bones asked. Jade ignored him.

"That's not the way it happened, I swear." Grizzly raised his hands in mock surrender. "I just helped with the escape."

"He's telling the truth," Bones said. "We're here because once again, Maddock has stepped in it."

"This can't be good." Jade folded her arms. "I'm listening."

"You know about the Sisterhood?" Bones asked.

Jade's eyebrows shot up. "They are involved?" She gave a shake of her head, took a step back, and swung the door open wide. "I was going to ask if you were keeping this pair out of trouble," she said to Spenser, "but I think that question has been answered. You'd all better come inside."

Jade's office was decorated with Polynesian art and artifacts and weapons. Her diplomas and awards hung on the wall behind her desk. Books were stacked two high and two deep on every shelf of the bookcases that lined one wall. The subject matter was varied, reflecting Jade's wide-ranging fieldwork. There were no photographs, no personal mementos. Typical Jade.

"Is it okay if I come in, too?" Grizzly asked from the doorway,

"Sure," Jade said. "Fair warning, if you pitch me another project while you're here, I'm going to punch you in the tackle."

"I think I almost like her," Spenser whispered in Maddock's ear.

"She's okay as long as you're on her good side."

Jade limped over to her desk and motioned for the others to sit. Several folding chairs stood in one corner. They all grabbed one and arrayed themselves opposite Jade.

"Not the most comfortable seats," Bones said.

"That's by design. I like to keep my meetings as short as possible. Now, tell me your story."

Bones began to fill her in. When he described Maddock's escape, Jade held up her hand to stop him.

"You took someone's Bronco without asking?" she said to Maddock. "I thought you disapproved of such things." Jade had once taken Maddock's vehicle in a moment of ned.

"Touché," Maddock said.

Bones continued on with the story. When he came to the end, Jade stared at him for a full five seconds.

"It was you who buzzed the *Arizona*? I should have known. What did you do with the plane?"

"Grizzly knew a place," Bones said. "It's hidden for the moment, but when it's found, it won't point to us."

"Who will it point to?" Jade asked.

Bones covered a fake cough. Everyone turned to stare at Maddock. He suddenly felt hot and itchy.

"What am I missing?" Jade asked.

"Isla Mulheron appears to be in charge," Maddock said

hoarsely. "That's who abducted me and we're confident that's who provided the plane to Grizzly."

Jade was momentarily dumbstruck, then broke into laughter. Bones quickly joined in. Jade took a moment to compose herself, wiped her eyes.

"That's the funniest thing I've heard in weeks, maybe years. Your ex-girlfriend kidnaps you, so you come to me for help."

"It wasn't funny at the time," Maddock said.

"You got away safely, so I'm allowed to laugh," Jade sat up straight, suddenly all business. "You're telling me you actually found the tomb of Kamehameha the Great."

"I did. And he was holding this." Maddock took the cylinder out of his backpack and handed it to her. "I think it's a Sumerian cylinder seal."

"What is a cylinder seal?" Grizzly asked. He was recording video with his smartphone.

"In many Middle Eastern cultures, a royal seal or some other image would be inscribed on a stone cylinder. You could brush ink on the outside of the cylinder and roll the image onto a flat surface like parchment." Jadee held it up to the light. "It's strange, though. There's nothing carved on this one. And it's much larger than any I've seen."

"I'll bet that's the first time she's ever said that to you, Maddock," Bones said.

"Screw you, Bones," Maddock said.

Jade gasped. Her eyes were aglow. She sprang from her seat, let out a grunt of pain, and sat back down. "I keep forgetting about my ankle."

"You figured something out?" Maddock asked.

"I just realized what else is wrong. The seal always had a hole drilled down the center so a cord could be threaded through, and it could be worn like a necklace. This one is capped at both ends."

"Let me see." Bones snatched the cylinder and gave one

end a twist. It spun free with surprising ease. "It's not capped anymore."

"Bones, you have got to stop doing that," Jade said. "We don't know what's in there."

Bones looked inside. "Looks like a golden scroll."

"Give it to me now," Jade said through gritted teeth. Bones handed it over. Jade looked inside, sucked in a sharp breath. "He's right."

From her desk, she took a pair of rubber-tipped tweezers, linen gloves, and a pair of reading glasses. Everyone gathered in close. Grizzly and Spenser were both recording on their smartphones, but Jade didn't notice. She donned the gloves, then cast a challenging glance at Bones as she slipped on the reading glasses.

"They're strictly for magnification."

"I didn't say anything," Bones said.

"Are they always like this?" Spenser asked.

"Actually, this is the best I've ever seen them get along. Jade hasn't thrown a single knife."

Jade held the cylinder in the light of her desk lamp. Maddock saw a glint of gold.

"This is like *National Treasure*," Spenser whispered.

"Yeah, but I'm much better-looking than Nic Cage," Bones said. "And Maddock's not quite as wimpy as his sidekick."

Jade took a long look at the object inside the cylinder, touched it with the tip of the tweezers. "It's solid." A hush fell over the group as she used the tweezers to slide the object free and hold it out for the others to see. It was a scroll about three inches wide, covered in fine, regular rows of text.

"It's Greek," Maddock said. "Can you read it?"

"I could translate it, but I can't sight-read. I do recognize a few words. 'Alexander Zeus-Ammon.'"

Bones whistled.

"Who the hell is Alexander Zeus-Ammon?" Grizzly

asked.

"You might know him better," Bones said, "as Alexander the Great."

Jade continued to scrutinize the golden scroll. Her lips moved as she struggled to read the ancient text.

"No way," she finally whispered. She turned to the others, eyes filled with wonder. "I think I know what this is."

15

"**I think this** is taken from a book called *History of Alexander's Conquests*. It was written by Ptolemy Soter and has been lost in its original form for over a thousand years." Jade's voice trembled.

"That explains the mask," Bones said.

"Mask?" Jade asked sharply.

"I was getting to it," Maddock said. "Kamehameha was wearing Ptolemy's death mask."

"That would be pertinent information," Jade said with exaggerated patience.

"What do you mean the book is lost in its original form?" Grizzly asked.

"Scholars used it as a primary source and quoted from it extensively, so fragments of it have survived. Attempts have been made to reassemble the available source material, but there's always debate over the authenticity of various extracts."

"Why is this written on gold?" Spenser asked.

"It's not gold per se, more like an amalgam of paper and gold. I've never seen its like. Whatever is written here, I'm sure it's important."

"Kamehameha was laid to rest with three treasures, all connected to Alexander the Great," Maddock said. "What's the connection?"

"Not many people know this, but late in life, Kamehameha became obsessed with Alexander. He sent envoys all over the world to collect legends and acquire artifacts and ancient texts. For some odd reason, he was highly secretive about it. Only a select few were aware."

"Why would he keep that a secret?" Spenser asked.
"Countless leaders have been fascinated with Alexander. It's

almost a cliché."

"He seemed to be focusing on one particular aspect of Alexander's legend—his hunt for the 'River of Paradise', a river that allegedly had healing powers."

"This would make a great documentary." Grizzly took a step back when Jade glared at him. "Sorry, can't help myself."

"Obviously," Jade said.

"Did Alexander find the river?" Bones asked.

"According to some accounts, he found a small pool of water that the locals held sacred. He put a dead fish into the water, and it came back to life. But most legends hold that he died without finding the river he sought, or he did find it and took the secret to his grave."

Spenser was furiously tapping away at her phone. Maddock knew she was taking notes for a future television show, but he was not going to let Jade in on that secret.

"Eden was supposed to be a paradise," Spenser said. "Do you think there might be a connection?"

Jade nodded. "In one Hebrew folk tale, Alexander found the river and followed its ever-narrowing path all the way to the gates of Eden. There, the river surged through a narrow crevice. Beside it stood a golden door. When Alexander knocked, he was greeted by the guardian of Eden, who declared him unworthy to enter because he had brought strife to the world instead of peace."

"No mention of keys to Eden?" Maddock asked.

"Not that I've heard of."

"Maybe that's the story told in the scroll," Bones said.

"Have you ever heard of a legend associated with Alexander's eyes?" Maddock scratched his head, trying to remember the odd rhyme Isla had recited. "Brown for the earth and blue for the sky."

Jade cocked her head. "Historians believe Alexander had a condition called heterochromia. One brown eye, one blue."

"The gemstone Lark called a key to Eden looked like an eye. It was amber with a golden iris. The pupil was a vertical slit."

"Maybe Alexander's blue and brown eyes were a pair of gemstones," Bones suggested, "like the Urim and Thummin in the Hebrew temple."

Jade frowned thoughtfully and nodded. "I'm always surprised when you say something intelligent."

"Thanks."

Jade gazed at the far wall, absently twirled a lock of hair around her finger as she thought. Finally, she nodded. "Some scholars will tell you Alexander was more than a conqueror. He was on a quest."

"A quest for what?" Grizzly asked.

"He wanted to be divine. To that end, he sought out anything that might help him attain that goal: lost treasures and items of power, forbidden or supposedly magical places. Everywhere he conquered, he studied their myths and legends, and searched for their most secret places. The Fountain of Youth, the Green Man, even paradise itself."

Maddock stood and began to pace around the small office, trying to piece together the clues they had so far.

"Alexander found two eye-shaped gems, one blue and one brown, which the Tuatha believe are keys to the land of Eden, where they will find a treasure."

"Never heard of a treasure associated with Eden," Jade said.

"Kamehameha was wearing Ptolemy's death mask, which could only have come from Ptolemy's tomb," Maddock continued. "And I'll wager that's also where Kamehameha found the amber eye."

"Ptolemy was Alexander's most trusted general," Jade said. "But he was also locked in a power struggle with the rest of Alexander's inner circle. It wouldn't be surprising if he kept one of the stones for himself as a symbol of power and a reminder to others of his connection to Alexander. He buried the other with Alexander."

Bones pounded his fist into his palm and let out a whoop.

"What was that for?" Jade asked.

"Are you kidding me? I've been fascinated with the story of Alexander's lost tomb for as long as I can remember."

"I'll document every step of the search!" Grizzly said, upending his chair as he sprang to his feet. "We'll call it, The Quest for Eden."

"Eden Quest sounds better." Jade frowned, stared at the door.

"What's wrong?" Maddock asked.

She lowered her voice to a whisper. "I think someone is listening outside."

16

"Keep talking," Maddock mouthed to Spenser. He didn't want the eavesdropper to suspect anything was amiss.

"What's the deal with Alexander's lost tomb? I always assumed it was in Alexandria." Spenser said.

"It was and it might still be," Jade replied.

"That's cryptic."

Maddock stood and moved quietly toward the door. He could see a shadow. Someone was definitely standing just outside Jade's office.

"Alexander's body was to have been interred in Macedonia, his birthplace," Jade said. "But Ptolemy's forces seized the body."

"Why?" Spenser asked.

"Symbolic power. Ptolemy ruled Egypt so he wanted to keep the body in the country. Alexander was first interred at Memphis until it could be moved to a lavish tomb in Alexandria where it remained on display for hundreds of years, first inside a coffin of gold that was fitted to his body, later in a coffin of glass or crystal. It survived a series of earthquakes and disasters, and the city was built up around and eventually above it until only a select few knew its location. But, by the end of the fourth century, no one could find the tomb. The last known record of it dates to 390 AD."

"How could it just disappear?" Spenser asked.

"At that time, Emperor Theodosian issued a series of decrees banning the practice of pagan religions and Christians used it as an excuse to eradicate as many pagan religious symbols as possible. Much like the Taliban today, they destroyed art, architecture, holy sites, anything they considered pagan."

"What happened to the tomb?" Grizzly asked.

"There are three schools of thought. The prevailing idea is that the Christians looted the tomb and destroyed Alexander's body, probably burned it. Another possibility is the body was moved somewhere deep beneath Alexandria where only those in the know could find it. The third possibility is that it was removed to a secret location."

Maddock frowned. Although the story Jade told was common knowledge, the figure at the doorway was not moving. *They're wondering if we know something they don't.* He glanced at Bones. There was a twinkle in his eye that said the two men were thinking the same thing.

"Let's cut to the chase," Bones said. "I can tell you exactly where the tomb is."

Jade frowned, but then her eyes met Maddocks' and she seemed to understand.

"I can't wait to hear this," she said sardonically. "Let me guess—it's beneath Loch Ness."

"Not even close, but Maddock and I could tell you a few stories about Nessie." Bones cleared his throat. "When Theodosian passed his decrees, the members of the cult of Alexander saw the writing on the wall. Alexander referred to himself as Zeus-Ammon, and he was worshiped in Egypt as a son of the god Amun the Egyptian equivalent of Zeus. They knew his tomb would be a prime target for religious zealots. So, they moved his body."

Bones paused for dramatic effect. The figure on the other side of the door didn't move.

Spenser sighed deeply. "Are you going to tell us what they did with it?"

"The Siwa Oasis, near the Libyan border," Bones said. "It's the place where Alexander was deified by the oracle, and there was a shrine there devoted to Amun."

"That's a thin shred of evidence," Jade said.

"There's more. Back in the eighties, archaeologists uncovered lion statues guarding the entryway to a large,

Hellenistic royal tomb. Inscriptions at the site discuss the transportation of a body."

"That turned out to be a dead end," Jade said. "Just a tomb built for someone of Ptolemy's royal family."

"It was a coverup. Authorities in Egypt and Greece started fighting over the tomb before it could be opened. Finally, the Egyptian government shut down the dig and reburied the tomb. Then they put out a fake story to hide the truth."

"I could probably get a permit to film on the site," Grizzly mused. "It could take some time."

In the gap beneath the doorway, Maddock saw the shadow disappear as the eavesdropper turn to walk away. He threw open the door, reached out, and snatched the spy by the wrist. The spy was a well-dressed young woman wearing a university ID badge that read *Kaiana Kane, Media Specialist*.

"Oh my God, what are you doing?" she cried.

"Kaiana? Why were you lurking outside my door?" Jade asked.

Kaiana flinched at the accusation. "I wasn't. I mean, it wasn't me. There was a woman standing at your door when I turned the corner, but she walked away as soon as she saw me coming her way." She pointed down the hall to an exit door. "I was suspicious at first, but then I heard voices and assumed you were in a meeting. I was trying to make up my mind whether to interrupt or email you when this guy grabbed me." She rubbed her wrist and stared daggers at Maddock.

"If someone absolutely insists on interacting with me, email is always best," Jade said.

"What did the woman look like?" Maddock said.

"I didn't see her face. Black hair, pale skin. Not a kanaka— you know, someone with island ancestry."

Maddock frowned. Isla knew about his history with

Jade. She might have sent Lark to spy. He ran down the hallway and through the exit door.

Outside was a manicured grass oval ringed by palm trees, hibiscus, and snowbush. Students were sitting or lying on the grass, studying, or chatting. In the middle, a group of young men and women kicked a soccer ball around. There was no sign of anyone fitting the description of Kaiana's spy.

"Are you lost?" a young woman sitting nearby called to him.

"Did a woman come this way? Black hair, pale skin."

The girl shook her head, but another of her companions perked up.

"Does she have purple eyes?"

"That's her," Maddock replied. Lark *had* been here!

"I saw her about a week ago. I only remembered because she looked so out of place."

"Where did you see her?"

"Coming out of the library. She looked angry about something. Almost ran me over."

"And you haven't seen her since?"

The young woman shook her head. Maddock thanked her and returned to Jade's office. Kaiana was hurrying away in the opposite direction.

"Friend of yours?" Maddock asked as he returned to his seat in Jade's office.

More like a colleague I don't yet want to stab," Jade said. "She doesn't talk too much, and she has good taste in movies, so we hang together from time to time."

"I take it the spy got away?" Bones asked.

"No sign of her. But someone fitting her description was seen in the library last week looking angry."

"Damn!" Grizzly swore. "If she heard what we were saying, that means the Sisterhood now knows the location of Alexander's tomb!"

"I thought you had more faith in me than that," Bones

said. "I had a look inside the Siwa tomb a few years back."

"How did you manage that?" Jade's eyes were wide with envy.

"I hooked up with a girl named Lily. Smoking hot, questionable morals. She was into black market antiquities and her group had bribed the right people. She let me come along when they breached the tomb. It was empty. No body, no artifacts, no clues. If Alexander was ever there, he's long gone."

"You never mentioned that," Maddock said.

"I didn't want to bring it up." Bones glanced away, looking abashed. "I'm pretty sure Lily was in the Illuminati."

"We can discuss your convoluted romantic life another day," Maddock says. "The Sisterhood has eyes on the college, which means we can't safely translate the scroll here." He turned to Jade. "Is there anywhere absolutely secure we can go?"

"I know a place," she said. "I'll drive."

17

The winding one-lane road wound along a cliff face. Flanked by rock on one side and a sheer drop on the other, Khekili Highway was one of Hawaii's most precarious drives. Running from Kapalu to Wailuku, the road was renowned for its narrow passages, snaking turns, and the occasional falling boulder.

"Nice view," Maddock said, looking out at the cerulean waters of the Pacific.

"You're only saying that because you can't see it from my angle," Bones complained from his position in the passenger seat. "I hope somebody brought snacks because it's going to be a long fall when Jade finally drives us off the cliff."

"How about I pull to the side and push you over?" Jade muttered, her eyes locked on the road ahead.

"Like there's room to pull over. This van is almost as wide as the road."

Operating on the assumption that the Sisterhood was tracking their movements, Jade had borrowed a maintenance van belonging to the college. Maddock, Grizzly, and Spenser sat in the back among barrels and boxes of cleaning supplies, while Jade drove, and Bones rode shotgun.

"Any time you want to get out, just open the door and take a flying leap," Jade said.

"I would but I forgot my parachute."

"Can we talk about something other than falling to our deaths?" Spenser said loudly.

"We could talk about the weather," Jade said. "There's a storm coming." Dark clouds loomed on the horizon.

"A wet road will be great for traction," Bones said.

"New topic," Spenser said firmly. "Let's talk about Alexander's tomb. If it's not at the oasis, where is it? Do you think the Christians destroyed it?"

"I believe it survived," Maddock said.

"What makes you so sure?" Grizzly asked.

"If even a fraction of the stories can be believed, the tomb of Alexander the Great was like no other. It was lined with gold and filled with treasures he accumulated in his conquests. Some accounts say his remains were encased in gold. Later, his body was placed inside a crystal coffin that allowed it to be viewed."

"Don't forget that Alexander's body was perfectly preserved," Bones said.

"Don't you mean mummified?" Spenser asked.

"I mean preserved like the day he died," Bones said.

"That's not possible," Grizzly said.

"It is if they got their hands on the right kind of Atlantean crystal," Bones said.

"Atlantean?" Grizzly demanded.

"Long story," Maddock said. "What's important is the Cult of Alexander worshiped him as a god, and his body and tomb were central to their faith. The tomb and the body were of great value materially and spiritually. The pagans could see which way the wind was blowing in the Roman Empire long before paganism was fully outlawed. No way they would risk Alexander and his treasure falling into the wrong hands. They must have taken steps to protect it."

"Makes sense." Grizzly sounded doubtful. "But how can we be sure the tomb *didn't* fall into the wrong hands in spite of their best efforts?"

"No artifacts from Alexander's tomb have been found, nor are there any legends to that effect," Maddock said.

"If it were me, and I'd managed to find and destroy the world's most famous Pagan tomb, I'd tell somebody," Bones said.

"You'd tell every somebody who would listen," Maddock replied.

"Exactly. And human nature hasn't really changed over the centuries." Bones turned to Grizzly. "If the tomb has been found, somebody would have talked."

"If I may interrupt," Jade said in a raised voice. "I think someone is following us."

Maddock looked back and saw a black Subaru tearing along the road, the driver showing no regard for the perilous circumstances. The vehicle was closing fast. Both passengers were women, the driver a brown-skinned woman with chestnut hair, the passenger a fair-skinned blonde. Maddock had never seen either of them before, but he thought he knew who had sent them.

"I recognize the driver. That's Meri. She was my 'host' at the resort. Someone should tell her the speed limit is fifteen miles per hour," Spenser said dryly.

"I don't think either of them cares."

"Maybe it's just someone in a hurry," Spenser said.

As if in reply, the passenger leaned out the window and aimed a pistol.

"Get down!" Maddock barked.

Jade understood the warning immediately. She yanked the wheel to the left an instant before the first shot rang out. The passenger side mirror exploded as the bullet struck it. The van missed the jagged gray rocks of the cliff wall by inches. Jade swore and yanked it back onto the narrow road.

"They don't need to shoot at us," Bones said. "Jade's driving is going to kill us."

"Like I said before, you can get out any time." Jade floored it and the van picked up speed as they chugged along. Jade continued to weave as much as the narrow road permitted.

Another shot rang out, and then a third. Both missed.

"Lucky us. She shoots like Maddock," Bones said.

"Hang on!" Jade shouted. An instant later, they hit a bump in the road. Maddock felt a tingling sensation as the van went airborne, and then the impact as the van hit the ground with a thud. "Remind me to tell the service department this thing needs new shocks."

Maddock looked back to see the shooter take aim again. A peal of thunder drowned out the report of the automatic pistol. Spenser let out a yelp as the slug slammed into the van's rear door.

"Are you hit?" Maddock said, reaching for her.

"No. I think the cleaning supplies saved us." She pointed to the stacks of boxes filled with powdered detergent.

"Maybe luck is on our side," Maddock said.

"I don't know about that," Jade said. "There's a hairpin turn up ahead. I'll have to slow down to a crawl to get around it without putting this thing on its side. We'll be sitting ducks."

"And it's starting to rain," Bones added. Fat droplets slapped the windshield and thudded on the roof. "Gonna be hard enough trying to stay on the road.

"I don't suppose we have any weapons of our own?" Grizzly asked.

"Sure, the university keeps a spare rocket launcher in every vehicle," Jade said. Grizzly's retort was lost when one of the van's small rear windows shattered, showering the cargo bay and its occupants with shards of safety glass. "Her aim is improving. Maddock, you've got to do something."

Maddock's eyes fell on the boxes of detergent. He grabbed one, ripped it open, and worked his way to the now-empty rear window. The Subaru was gaining on them, seemingly oblivious to the sharp turn ahead.

"Don't' slow down until I give the word," Maddock said, "and then I want you to hit the brakes hard."

"I can give you a few seconds."

"That's all I need."

The Subaru was close. The operative in the passenger seat leaned out of the window again.

"Get ready," Maddock said.

The blonde woman blinked the rain out of her eyes, gave her head a shake. She took aim again.

"Now!"

Maddock braced himself as Jade slammed on the brakes. A split second later, the driver of the Subaru also braked hard. The sudden lurch caused the shot to go wide. Maddock hurled the box of detergent out the window. It struck the vehicle on the hood and burst, sending up a cloud of powdered soap. In the light rain, the soap clung to everything it touched, including the windshield.

The Subaru skidded off to the side and struck the guard rail in a shower of sparks. The driver overcorrected, whipped the car back to the left. The vehicle fishtailed. Its rear quarter panel struck the cliff face and the Subaru went into a spin.

Maddock hoped it would spin right off the cliff, but no such luck. It came to a halt, facing the opposite direction. One tire was flat.

"That will slow them for a minute or two, but not much more than that," Maddock said. "Better step on it."

"The speed limit is literally five miles per hour on these turns," Jade said as she stepped on the gas.

"Since when are you a rule-follower?" Bones asked.

"Following the laws of physics is not a matter of personal choice. Now, hold on to your butts." Jade gritted her teeth and hit the gas.

"I can't believe you're quoting *Jurassic Park* right now," Bones said.

Jade's brow furrowed, her eyes locked on the road as they whipped around the blind curve. "What are you talking about?"

"Seriously?" Bones shook his head. "Just when I

thought there was hope for you."

Jade kept the van moving at a steady clip—too fast for conditions, not fast enough to keep them alive. The skies grew dark, and the rainfall grew heavier. Visibility was almost nil.

"This will make it harder for them to catch up with us," Spenser said, looking out at the curtains of gray rain.

"And harder for us to get away," Maddock said.

"I don't get your relationship. Do you two have anything at all in common?" Bones asked.

"We're yen and yang. That's what makes it work." Spenser gave Maddock a quick kiss on the cheek.

"If opposites attract, why hasn't Jade found somebody? She's everyone's opposite," Bones said.

Jade quirked an eyebrow, glanced up at the sky.

"Thanks a lot, Bones," she said. "You just proved God doesn't exist."

"How's that?"

"I've had cups of coffee that lasted longer than some of your relationships. If God were real, she would have struck you down with lightning for that bit of hypocrisy."

"That's fair," Bones said.

"And who says I don't have somebody?" Jade smiled mysteriously.

"Is it that Kaiana chick from the school? Is that why she was acting so weird?"

"She wishes. And I can't believe you're still calling women 'chicks.' We're not weak baby birds."

"Also, it's not 1972 anymore," Spenser added.

"What's contemporary slang for, 'they're back'?" Maddock said. In the distance, their pursuers had rounded the bend and were back on their tail.

They were running without headlights. The small, black vehicle looked like a shark closing in, cutting a V through the rainwater that flooded the narrow road.

"We're almost there," Jade said. "Can you buy us one more minute? Hell, I'll take thirty seconds."

"What difference will that make?" Bones asked.

"You'll see."

"Anyone got any bright ideas?" Bone asked.

"When I was a kid, we used to spread plastic tarps out on the hill in our backyard," Grizzly began.

"What the hell are you talking about?" Jade snapped. She whipped the van around another turn as another shot rang out.

"We'd turn on the garden hose, cover ourselves in dish soap, and slide down the hill."

Maddock understood immediately. "Grizzly, that's brilliant! You and Spenser start throwing these boxes out the back."

The pair immediately began tossing the boxes of cleaning powder out onto the road. Some broke open, spreading bubbles across the road. Others bounced and struck the pursuing vehicle, but the Subaru kept coming.

"Bones, help me with this barrel." A large barrel of concentrated liquid soap was strapped to the wall. If they could dump it out across the road just before the next turn…

"I got it," Bones said. "Just open the doors and get the hell out of the way." In a flash, he freed the heavy barrel and tipped it onto its side. "Open them now!

The tone of command got an immediate reaction. Grizzly flung the doors open and then flattened himself against the inside wall.

"Bones, I…" Maddock began.

Before he could finish, Bones heaved and sent the barrel rolling out the back door. It struck the pavement, bounced end over end, and flew into the air.

The driver of the Subaru had only a split second to react. She hit the brakes.

The barrel struck smashed into the windshield. The

little car veered off the road, crashed through the guardrail, and slid over the ledge. It bounded down the steep incline, tearing through the tangle of jungle growth that clung to the hill, and came to a halt halfway down the cliff, pinned between two palm trees.

"Seriously? How lucky can you get?" Bones said.

"Mother Nature rewards those who drive eco-friendly vehicles," Spenser said.

"Even trained assassins?" Maddock asked.

Spenser pointed at the Subaru as if that were all the proof she needed. The trees that held the two-door vehicle in place now had the occupants trapped. Maddock caught a glimpse of the driver pounding on her window before they rounded another turn and the vehicle disappeared from his line of sight.

Bones closed the doors, then turned to Maddock. "Sorry, Maddock. You were saying something earlier?"

"I was going to say I needed to open the plug on the barrel."

Bones frowned. "Why would you do that?"

Maddock closed his eyes and gave a shake of his head.

"Never mind, Bones. It's not important anymore."

They continued on, now driving at a rate of speed that didn't invite certain death. They had gone barely a mile when Jade took a sudden turn and drove the van off the road and into the jungle.

"Where the hell are we going?" Bones asked.

Jade grinned. "You'll see." She tapped a code into her phone and up ahead, in the middle of what had appeared to be an impenetrable wall of vegetation, a gate opened, revealing a narrow track winding its way into the jungle.

"Pretty cool," Bones said. "Who came up with that."

"Who do you think?" Jade said.

A small house came into view. A large satellite dish sat beside it. A familiar-looking man stepped out of the door and waved.

"No way." A grin spread across Bones' face. "Professor!"

18

Pete Chapman was a former comrade in the SEALs. He was nicknamed Professor for his quick mind and breadth of knowledge. He was a solid, reliable man who had had their backs on numerous missions, and even during some of their exploits after leaving the service.

"Are the two of you still working together?" Maddock asked.

"I haven't done any fieldwork in a while," Jade said. "But we hang out."

Maddock wondered what that meant. Was there something going on between the two? Not that it was any of his concern.

"Does that mean you two are hooking up?" Bones asked.

"None of your business," Jade said.

Professor's home was situated on a mountainside overlooking the Pacific. The interior was sparsely furnished, save for many bookshelves, but otherwise clean and neat. Exactly what Maddock would have expected. Professor led them through a living area that looked out from their mountainside down to the sea, and into a small room retrofitted to serve as a laboratory.

"Nice place," Spenser said.

Professor nodded in acknowledgment, but his mind was already on the task at hand. "Where is the scroll?"

Maddock took no offense at his old friend's abrupt manner. Professor's no-nonsense personality and his burning academic curiosity often gave him a one-track mind.

Maddock handed over the cylinder. Professor donned gloves and carefully removed the scroll, unrolled it, and laid it on a tabletop covered with plain white paper. He flicked on a bright lamp with a magnifying glass attached and inspected the artifact.

"I agree with Jade. The language appears to fit the time of Ptolemy."

"We can translate it, then?" Maddock asked.

"Jade and I can, but it will take some time." Professor took a step back, frowned. After a long pause, he ran his fingers across the scroll. "I would love to know what material this is made from. It looks and feels like gold, but it's light and flexible like no metal I've ever seen." He gave his head a quick shake. "But that's a problem for another day. We'll get started on the translation."

"What can we do to help?" Grizzly asked.

"You can start by reaching out to the Egyptian authorities on behalf of your show and request permission to film at Siwa Oasis," Maddock said.

"I thought Bones said there was nothing there."

"But Isla and her crew don't know that. If they've got ears inside the department of antiquities, we want them to think Siwa is our target." Maddock paused. "We should also reach out to Jimmy Letson. Maybe he can dig up something." Jimmy was an old friend and an accomplished hacker who helped them out from time to time.

"Way ahead of you," Professor said. "I called him up as soon as I got Jade's message. He said we were wasting our time. In his opinion, if the directions to the tomb were online, someone would have found them by now. But he's going to try."

"In the meantime," Maddock said, "the three of us can do some digging on our own. Often the clues are lying in plain sight, waiting to be discovered. Maybe something will turn up."

While Jade and Professor worked on translating the scroll, Maddock, Bones, and Spenser conducted their own research into the lost tomb. Maddock and Spenser focused on the tomb in Alexandria, while Bones delved into the more esoteric theories.

Alexander had been laid to rest in a place called the Soma, a walled enclosure in the royal district where the kings of the Ptolemaic line were entombed. Deep in the rock beneath the Soma was the tomb where the body of Alexander lay in state, surrounded by the trappings of extravagant wealth. Pilgrims visited the tomb, including several Roman emperors, but the accounts were sorely lacking in detail.

The Soma had been wiped out by a storm in the fourth century, but portions of the city and the wall that surrounded it remained for centuries. They found a Napoleonic-era map that showed the outline of the old city but no clues to the location of the tomb.

"I think we need a new angle," Spenser finally said. "We're looking at the same information searchers have pored over for over a thousand years."

"There was a network of underground canals beneath the Soma," Bones said. "If we could find them, Maddock and I could swim around and see what stumble over."

"I'd like something more to go on," Maddock said. He turned to Professor and Jade, who were scrutinizing the scroll and scribbling notes. "Any progress on the translation."

"A little," Jade said, not taking her eyes off her work.

"We haven't found any clues," Professor said. "So far, this is an account of Alexander's final expedition. We're a long way from his death."

"Why don't you translate from back to front?" Bones asked.

Professor grimaced and shook his head. "There's a right and wrong way to do things."

Maddock's phone vibrated. It was Jimmy.

"You owe me another bottle of Scotch," Jimmy said

without preamble.

"It was Professor who called you."

"Yeah, but it's for your project," Jimmy said.

"Found anything helpful?"

"I don't know. Augustus Caesar may or may not have broken off a piece of the mummy's nose." Jimmy paused. "Otherwise, the recorded visits to his tomb are mostly generic accounts written by historians long after the events had transpired."

"Mostly?" Maddock asked.

"I found one first-hand account, a journal entry by a ship's captain who bribed his way into the tomb. I think he fancied himself a poet. Listen to this." Jimmy cleared his throat and began to read.

"'*Dark clouds blanketed the sky. We crept along in darkness. When the fiery eye turned its gaze directly upon us, the needles cast long shadows, fingers clutching the entrance to the tomb.*' Sounds like a Tolkien wannabe." Jimmy barked a laugh. "I don't suppose that's of any use?"

"Actually, I think you're on to something." Maddock's heart raced. "The fiery eye has got to be the Great Lighthouse of Alexandria. And the three needles..."

"Cleopatra's Needles!" Bones exclaimed.

Cleopatra's Needles were a pair of obelisks that had stood in Alexandria for two thousand years before eventually being moved. One was now located in Central Park near the Metropolitan Museum of Art, the other in London on the bank of the Thames River. Unlike most of ancient Alexandria, the original site of the needles was well-known—their spot overlooking the harbor now occupied by a statue of Egyptian revolutionary Saad Zaghloul.

The lighthouse, one of the Seven Wonders of the Ancient World, had been built on an island called Pharos during the reign of Ptolemy II. For centuries it had served as a beacon to ships traveling to the Egyptian city. It was said its light could be seen as much as forty kilometers away. Eventually, a series of earthquakes destroyed it, and the remains were used to construct a fort on the site.

"Given that we know the original locations and heights of the lighthouse and the needles, could you make a projection of where their shadows would have touched?" Maddock asked Jimmy.

"The lighthouse had a revolving mirror," Bones said. "The shadows would make an arc."

"The account says the light was directly upon them," Maddock said. "What would a straight shot look like?"

"Depends on the intensity of the light," Jimmy said. Maddock could hear keys clicking away as his friend typed furiously. "I'll give it a shot." A few minutes later, he clapped his hands. "Yahtzee!"

"Nobody plays that game anymore," Bones said.

"I've mapped out the probable arc, as well as the direct path of the shadows," Jimmy went on. "And I overlaid it on a map of the modern city. I think we have a winner!"

"Where is it?"

"Sending you a map now."

A moment later, Maddock's phone buzzed again. He opened the attachment and smiled.

"Jimmy, you're a genius!" He turned to the others. "Looks like we're going to Alexandria!"

19

"That was Phyllis," Lark said, hanging up the phone. She heaved a tired sigh. "Our team failed."

"Can you be more specific?" Isla's nerves were stretched thin, and she was growing fed up with Lark's vague comments and secretive nature. The woman worked for her, yet she behaved as if she operated independently.

"Meri and Briony staked out Don Ho College. Jade Ihara tried to smuggle Maddock and his friends out in a university van. There was a chase." Lark grimaced.

"And?" Isla raised her eyebrows.

"There was an accident. Briony and Meri went over a cliff. They weren't able to free themselves before the authorities arrived."

"And Maddock?"

"He got away. But my contact at the college is going to try and connect with Ihara, figure out where they went."

"Who is this contact of yours?"

"She works in the library. I first met her while looking for information on Kamehameha. It was a stroke of luck that she's friends with Maddock's ex." Lark paused, flashed a mischievous grin. "Sorry. *One* of his exes."

"Can we stick to business?" Isla snapped. Ever since Maddock came into the picture, it seemed she and Lark couldn't have a conversation without the woman trying to draw her into "girl talk."

"Touchy," Lark said. "Fine. Here's the sitrep. Maddock is in the wind. Briony and Meri are in custody charged with reckless driving, but they're not suspected of anything else. Phyllis is alive and awaiting further instructions."

"Is there any good news?" Isla asked.

"Perhaps. I just learned that Grizzly Grant has applied

for a permit to film at Siwa Oasis."

"Brilliant!" Isla said. "So, we're on the right track." She looked around. "I hope our guide gets here before the permit is issued."

"He's only five minutes late. Don't be so dramatic."

Isla smirked. Even if Grant knew which strings to pull and which palms to grease, the permit wouldn't be issued overnight. Still, she preferred to work with people she could count on. Unfortunately, the world of black market antiquities was filled with flighty characters.

The tour was nearing its end when she felt a tug at her sleeve. She turned to see a small man with leathery skin and silver hair smiling up at her.

"Can you spare a coin?" he whispered.

It took her a moment to remember this was a planned greeting, a way of the man identifying himself without revealing his business.

"Yes, but only one," she replied.

Satisfied, the small man nodded and tilted his head in the direction of the car park. The three of them slipped away from the crowd, not that anyone was paying attention. Before they reached their vehicle, he made a sharp turn and led them into a forest of palm trees. Once out of sight, he stopped.

"I am Chisis," he said simply. "You have the money?"

Lark counted out five hundred Egyptian pounds and handed them over. The bills vanished into one of the many pockets of his cargo pants.

"As much again if we find what we are looking for," Lark said.

"I know the way," Chisis assured them. With that, he turned and stalked off into the trees.

The sun was setting when they came to a halt at a narrow ravine. Chisis pointed down.

"It is not far from here, but the path is difficult. We will have to climb down, crawl for a short distance, and then climb up again."

"I don't understand," Isla said. "I thought the tomb lay beneath a temple."

"It does," Chisis said. "But it is under surveillance at all times. This is what you would call the back door."

"All right. You first," Lark said. "And if you are leading us into a trap…"

"No, Miss. Not at all." Chisis raised his hands. "I promise you this is the way. I will lead."

As their guide had promised, the way was difficult. They belly-crawled into a tiny opening beneath a rock and scooted forward until they reached a place where they could stand. They stood at the base of a wide cleft in the rock.

"The builders had a back passageway that was sealed up after construction," Chisis explained. "But some years ago, an earthquake opened up a way into the passageway."

They took their time scaling the cliff. Isla's heart was in her throat. They already had one of the eyes, enough, according to legend, to cross the barrier into Eden. But she wanted them both.

They emerged in a broad passageway with a low ceiling. To their right, fallen rubble barred their way. To their left, a stone door was set in the wall. Symbols were carved all around, but there was neither handle nor hinge.

"This is the door," Chisis said, shining his light on it.

"Open it," Lark said.

"I am sorry, but I assumed you would know how," Chisis said.

The fingers of Lark's right hand twitched. The woman was always carrying concealed, and she was far too eager to reach for her weapon.

"Let me take a look." Isla examined the symbols. One leaped out at her immediately. An eight-pointed star—the Star of Macedon.

"This was a symbol associated with Alexander the Great." She gave it a close inspection. Unlike the other symbols, the lines were cut deep into the rock. She worked her fingers inside and gave it a turn. Grudgingly, the handle spun a quarter turn, and the door swung back on invisible hinges.

"Remarkable!" Lark whispered.

They entered the tomb, but when the beams of their flashlights played around the large open space, Isla's heart sank. The walls were carved with scenes from Alexander's life. A bier stood at the center of the space, but nothing lay atop it.

"He's gone," Lark said.

"I don't believe he was ever here," Isla said, looking around.

"Why do you say that?" Lark asked.

"His tomb in Alexandria was opulent. Perhaps this was intended to eventually become his permanent resting place, but I can't see them laying him to rest in such a simple tomb."

Lark's shoulders bounced in silent mirth.

"What's funny?"

"I'm imagining all the effort Grizzly Grant is going to put into a project that is doomed to failure."

Isla considered this for a moment, then clapped her hand to her forehead. "I am a gommy."

"How many times do I have to tell you, I don't know your Scottish slang?"

"I'm a fool. Grant is a buffoon, but Maddock is clever enough to suspect we have spies inside the department of antiquities. If he believed Alexander's body was here, he would never have allowed Grant to go through official channels."

"What is that sound?" Chisis said. Isla had forgotten he was there, and she jumped at the sound of his voice.

They paused, listened. And then a door at the far end of the tomb swung open. They saw lights and the silhouettes of a man and woman in uniform.

"We've been set up!" Lark drew her pistol and fired four shots. The officers went down.

"You bloody bampot! A break-in at an empty tomb will soon be forgotten. Killing two officers guarantees they won't stop searching for us. Why did you do that?"

Lark shrugged, turned, and shot Chisis in the heart. The little man let out a tiny gasp. His eyes went wide, and he slumped to the ground. He lay there, gazing up at the ceiling through sightless eyes.

"It wasn't me. It was him." Lark wiped her pistol clean, then pressed it into the fallen man's hand.

Isla grimaced. Every day, Lark became more of a wild card.

20

The Cathedral of St. Mark stood a short distance from the waterfront in the center of what had once been ancient Alexandria. It was built in the Coptic style, blending Egyptian building traditions and materials with Graeco-Roman and Christian Byzantine motifs. At the entrance, six white columns supported a sandstone arch surmounted by a cross. A pair of minarets—small narrow towers, loomed above. It was smaller than Maddock had expected but elegant in its simplicity.

"We're sure this is the place?" Spenser asked, looking around at the buildings that surrounded them. The city had closed in on all sides of the ancient church. Now it was flanked by a seminary on one side and residential buildings on the other.

"According to Jimmy's calculation, this is where the shadows of Cleopatra's Needles would have pointed," Maddock said. "And it was customary practice for the early Christians to not only absorb Pagan holidays into their worship, but to build places of worship on sites Pagans already held sacred."

Spenser nodded doubtfully. She looked like she wanted to say more, but just then, three young women, a blonde, a brunette, and a redhead, approached.

"You're Spenser Saroyan!" the brunette exclaimed. "We love your travel vids. Can we get a pic with you?"

Spenser posed with each of the young women in turn. Grizzly, who appeared miffed at not having been recognized, assumed camera duty. He had just finished the blonde suddenly cocked her head to the side and gaped.

"It's you!" she said.

"It's me," Grizzly said, grinning.

"Not you." She brushed past the television presenter and stalked toward a sheepish-looking Bones, anger burning in her big green eyes. "I'm talking about this jerk. We spent a wonderful night together in Peru and he never called me again."

"If I had a dollar for every time I heard that," Maddock whispered to Spenser.

"Sorry," Bones said. "I travel a lot. How have you been?"

"Like you care." She thrust out her lower lip. "You owe me dinner. Are you free tonight?"

"Sorry, but I can't. We're working."

"You're on a treasure hunt? What are you looking for? Is it somewhere in the church?"

"Keep your voice down," Bones said. "I'm in a competitive business. Somebody might be spying on us right now."

"I'll keep quiet if you'll promise to call me later."

"Deal. Give me your number."

"You already have it." Her eyebrows shot up. "Hold on. Do you even remember my name?"

"I'm really bad with names," Bones admitted.

"It's Carly."

"Right!" Bones smiled. "I remember now. You have a birthmark on your…"

Carly slapped him. Not hard, but sharply enough to shut him up.

"On second thought, don't call me." With that, she turned on her heel and stalked away. Her friends followed, casting baleful stares at the tall man as they walked away.

"What do I look like to her, an *Oscar's* host?" Bones complained, rubbing his cheek.

They climbed the steps and passed through the double doors and into the cathedral. Maddock noticed that some visitors paused to kiss the door before they entered. They were greeted by a pair of brightly-colored mosaics—one depicting Mary, the other Saint Mark. Three rows of mahogany brown wooden pews filled the sanctuary, exquisite crystal chandeliers dangled from the high vaulted ceiling. On the opposite end, another mosaic, the Last Supper, looked down from the eaves onto the congregants.

Upon the altar stood the Seat of Saint Mark—a wooden chair with velvet cushions. The armrests were affixed to the backs of two wooden lions.

"The lion was the symbol of Saint Mark," Maddock explained.

They wandered the cathedral, drifting along with the other tourists, admiring the art and architecture. They saw the relics of Saint Mark—a few items inside a transparent case.

In the corner of one of the transepts, a marble slab was engraved with the names of all the popes that were buried on the site, along with the date they were interred.

"Saint Mark the Evangelist, in the year sixty-three," Grizzly read aloud, a note of wonder in his voice. "It's strange to think of him as a real person."

"I feel the same way about Bones," Spenser said.

"We're in a church. Be nice," Bones chided.

The list was numbered, and something caught Maddock's eye.

"The number fifty is missing." He pointed to the bottom of the slab. "Pope Mark is forty-nine, Simon fifty-one. No fifty."

"I guess a sculptor can't hit 'Control-Z'." Spenser paused, an expectant look on her face. "Come on! That was funny." Finally, she rolled her eyes and gave a shake of her head. "Anyway, the number fifty is missing because Pope James, the fiftieth Pope of Alexandria, is buried elsewhere."

Bones raised his eyebrows. "How do you know that?"

"I've been reading up on the cathedral and its history.

Haven't you?"

"No, I prefer the blank slate approach."

"So, where is your empty mind telling us to go next?" Spenser asked. "Because I haven't seen anything promising inside the church."

"Into the catacombs." Bones pointed at the ground.

"Isn't that kind of obvious?" Grizzly asked.

"This church was destroyed and rebuilt centuries ago," Maddock explained. "If we're going to find anything, most likely it will be underground."

The catacombs were accessed through a pair of glass doors nearby. A sign taped to the door read, CATACOMBS CLOSED. The line below it was written in Arabic. Spenser tried the handle, but the door would not budge.

"Dammit, it's locked," she said.

"Do you hear that Maddock? The door is locked." Bones said, a note of amusement in his voice. "I guess we should book our flights home." He let out a grunt as Spenser punched him in the biceps.

"You don't have to be an ass all the time," she hissed.

"I kind of do. Good punch, by the way." He gave her a condescending pat on the shoulder, then moved to a table where he found a stack of guidebooks held together by a fat paper clip. Bones stole the clip and, while the others kept watch, used it to pick the lock.

"That was fast," Maddock said.

"Simple lock. This isn't exactly a maximum security facility." He swung open the door. "Ladies and gentlemen, welcome to your private tour of the catacombs. Don't forget to tip your guide." He and Maddock stepped through. Spenser and Grizzly followed and locked the door behind them.

A red carpeted staircase led down into the lower levels. A mosaic depicting events from the life of Saint Mark covered three walls. They came to a smaller, narrower set of stairs that took them past a wrought iron door and deeper underground.

Beyond an arched doorway was a tunnel lined with blue tiles interspersed with tiny gold crosses. Maddock felt like he was moving back in time with each step. The air was damp, cold, and musty.

At the end of the passageway hung a painting of Saint Mark. The apostle looked down upon a meter-high trapdoor, plexiglass in a metal frame, set in the wall. On the other side was the foundation of the old church. Through a hole in the wall, they could see the ancient stone wall that barred the way to the catacombs.

"That's it?" Spenser said.

"Only if you're a rule-follower." Bones proceeded to unlock the small door. "Think Maddock can squeeze his fat butt through?"

It was a tight fit, but Maddock managed to work his way through. Spenser and Grizzly followed. Then came Bones, who managed to get himself stuck, one shoulder in, one shoulder out.

"He looks like Winnie the Pooh when he got stuck in the honey tree," Spenser said.

"How did he get out?" Grizzly asked.

"They left him there until he lost weight." She glanced at Bones. "I guess we'll see you in about two weeks?"

"Screw you guys. Help me get out of here." With much grunting and swearing, the big Cherokee was dragged through the trapdoor. He stood, gingerly rubbed his chest. "You guys didn't have to be so rough."

"That's what she said," Maddock and Spenser chimed in unison.

Bones glared at them. "You guys are the worst couple ever."

"The catacombs are sealed," Grizzly said from behind them. He was standing before the wall, running his fingers across the ancient stone. "Can we break it down?"

"I don't think we'll need to." Maddock gave the wall a close inspection, then took a few steps back.

"What are you looking for?" Spenser asked.

"There's no way the church would seal up the tombs and not leave themselves a way to get back in." He narrowed his eyes. And then he saw it. A rectangular patch where the mortar was a slightly different shade of gray. Viewed from just the right angle, it formed the outline of a doorway.

The bottom stone jutted out about an inch. Maddock slid his fingers under it and felt around. He found a set of indentations, perfectly spaced for the fingers of two hands. He took hold and lifted. Slowly, the section of wall rose about a half an inch and then swung back. Beyond was a crumbling passageway. Vaults ran along both sides of the wall. Each had a Roman numeral above it.

Maddock took the lead as they made their slow way into the crypt. The first tomb they encountered was numbered I.

"This is the tomb of Saint Mark," Bones said. "Hard to believe it's real."

There was no time for sightseeing. They searched the catacombs, examining each vault for anything unusual, symbols that might be associated with Alexander the Great. They were approaching the far end of the crypt when something caught Maddock's eye.

"I thought you said the fiftieth pope was buried somewhere else," he said to Spenser.

"He was," she replied.

Maddock shone his light on the capital L carved above the nearest vault.

"Then why is there a vault number fifty?"

21

Maddock gave the vault a closer inspection. There were no markings anywhere on it. No name or date. Just the Roman numeral above it marking it number fifty.

"Maybe they built it for the fiftieth pope before he died?" Grizzly offered.

"Maybe," Maddock said doubtfully. "Something tells me there's more to it than that."

He ran his fingers over the door. It was smooth, covered in a thin layer of grime. At the top of the vault door, he felt something—grooves and curves carved into the rock. He wiped away layers of dust that had accumulated over the centuries. He stepped back and shone his light on the spot.

"There's something there, but I can't quite make it out."

"It's a peacock! Look here." Grizzly moved to the door and traced his finger along the shallow grooves, outlining the body and the array of feathers. As soon as he pointed it out, Maddock could see it.

"It is said that the first time Alexander the Great saw peacocks, he was overwhelmed by their magnificence that he forbade anyone to kill them. He said they were 'worthy of the gods' attention.' He even adopted the peacock feather as a symbol of his power," Maddock said.

"Wouldn't that just call attention to the fact that his tomb is down there?" Spenser asked.

"Maybe not. The Christian church also assumed the peacock as a symbol of the pope's power." He moved closer, focused his light on the eye. There was a pattern inside it, but difficult to make out. "I wish I had a brush," he said.

"Makeup brush okay?" Spenser asked, digging into her fanny pack. A moment later, she handed over a small brush. "If this works, you have to stop making fun of me about my makeup."

"Deal."

Maddock used the brush to carefully clear away the rest of the dirt from the peacock's eye. Little by little, the image revealed itself. An eight-pointed starburst.

"This is the symbol of Alexander the Great." As the others moved in for a closer look, he handed the brush back to Spenser. "Looks like you win the bet."

"For the record, I did not agree to the bet," Bones said. He frowned. "How do we get it open?"

"The eye is the key. Rather, it's the keyhole."

"What's that supposed to mean?"

Maddock placed the tip of his thumb against the eye, thumbnail pressed into the groove. He said a silent prayer, pressed the eye, and twisted. He breathed a sigh of relief as the eye slowly rotated a half-turn to the right and locked into place.

Three loud knocks resounded through the quiet crypt. And then the door began to sink into the floor.

"Are you getting this?" Grizzly asked.

"Have you met me?" Spenser was recording it all on her smartphone.

"I really hate to be that guy, but in these situations, we usually like to have both hands free and our eyes focused on something other than a screen," Maddock said.

"I'll be careful," Spenser replied in a voice that said she wasn't really listening.

Beyond the door lay an empty vault. When they stepped inside, a door set in the far wall slid open. Beyond was a narrow passageway and at the far end, a large chamber. The beam of Maddock's flashlight caught a glimmer of gold.

No sooner had they moved into the passageway than the door slammed behind them. They searched for a release mechanism.

"No joy," Bones said.

"We'll just have to find another way out," Grizzly proclaimed. "Let's get this on camera." He turned and strode down the corridor.

They reached an arched doorway and paused to look inside. They shone their lights around the room. Spenser gasped, Grizzly whistled, and Bones whispered a curse.

The walls and ceiling were gold, the floor covered in sparkling blood-red tiles. Weaponry from the time of Ancient Greece adorned the walls. At the center of the room, a glass case stood atop a bier made of black obsidian. They couldn't see inside, but there was an air of certainty about what they would find.

"You first, Maddock," Bones said. "You found it, after all. It's only fair."

"Bullshit. We'll all go together."

As they approached, they saw the foundation upon which the coffin lay was shaped like a four-pointed star. It had two levels, the top smaller than the bottom, forming steps leading up to the glass case.

When they reached the case, they were rendered mute. A withered mummy lay inside the glass. His robes were crumbling. Remnants of dried flowers lay in dust at the bottom of the glass coffin. He wore a thick gold chain around his neck.

"The tip of his nose is broken," Bones said.

"According to legend, Emperor Augustus brought the mummy out, decorated it with flowers, and accidentally broke the nose off." Maddock was bitterly disappointed. This was not at all what he had expected.

Lark and Isla stood outside Saint Mark's Cathedral in Alexandria. They kept out of sight, scanning the crowd for signs of Maddock and his team. Lark wouldn't mind seeing Maddock again. Their time together had been all too short.

"You are certain Maddock is here?" Isla asked for at least the fourth time.

"His girlfriend is here. Someone tagged her in a photo on social media. And if she's here, I'll wager Maddock is close by." Lark frowned. "I'm surprised he's into that type of girl."

"What type? Blonde, beautiful, and successful?" Isla grumbled. "Every time she posts a selfie with Maddock in the shot, I feel like clubbing a baby seal."

"You follow her on social media? I thought you had no interest." Isla's blush was all Lark needed to know she was right. "You created a fake profile, didn't you?"

"I couldn't use my own name, could I?" Isla said.

"I follow her," Lard said. "It's funny, she and Maddock sort of look alike. That's kind of creepy, don't you think?"

"New subject." Isla took a deep breath. "Keep an eye out for his friend Bonebrake. He's likely to be a head taller than anyone else in the building, and almost certainly the only Native American."

Lark suddenly perked up. "There's the girl who made the post. Hold on." She approached a group of young women, spoke briefly with them, and hurried back. "According to those girls, Spenser, Bonebrake, and two friends went inside the church and haven't returned," she confirmed.

They entered the church and wandered along with the tourists, pretending to admire the architecture and the relics of Saint Mark the Evangelist. They covered the entire chancel but there was no sight of Maddock.

"Surely he hasn't left already," Lark mused.

"Don't give up so soon," Isla replied. "If he's looking for

Alexander's Tomb, he will most likely look underground." She pointed down. "There are catacombs underneath the church."

"Why didn't you say so?" Lark rolled her eyes. "Let's go."

They found the door to the catacombs, and a sign informing visitors that the catacombs were closed. As they approached, a tall priest rushed past, unlocked the door, and hurried through.

"Wait here. Don't let anyone else through." Lark slipped through the door before Isla could argue with her. Isla was smart and determined, but she was terrible at stealth. Lark could check out the catacombs much faster by herself. And if she caught up to Maddock, she knew she had the willpower to do what needed to be done. She wasn't so certain about Isla's resolve.

She followed the sound of the priest's footsteps down two flights of stairs, through a passageway, to a place where a small opening led into the catacombs. The priest let out a gasp when he saw it open.

"Someone has been inside," he whispered. He plunged through the tiny door.

Lark stalked him, remained just out of sight as the priest hurried through the catacombs. When he reached tomb number fifty, he stopped short and let out a cry.

"It is open," he whispered aloud.

Lark decided it was time to make her presence known. She stepped out of the shadows and stalked toward the priest. He spotted her and his expression of surprise turned to one of outrage.

"What are you doing in here, *woman*?"

It was the emphasis he put on the word "woman" that led Lark to kick him in the groin. He let out a grunt and slumped to his knees. Lark drew her knife and pressed it to his cheek, just below his eye socket.

"Where were you going in such a hurry?" she asked. "And don't lie."

"A pretty blonde girl came down here."

"And you thought you'd try and get her alone down in the crypts?" Lark twisted the knife a quarter of a turn. A thin trickle of blood flowed down the priest's cheek.

"No, I mean, I don't know. She should not have been down here. The crypts are closed."

"This blonde, was she with anyone?"

"A man with wavy brown hair. I think I've seen him on television."

That would be Grizzly Grant. "Anyone else?"

"Not that I saw."

Lark glanced at the open tomb. It was empty. "What is the significance of this tomb? Was there a body here before?"

"I don't know. On my first day I was instructed that if I should ever see this tomb open, I should immediately step inside and press a specific stone." Sweat beaded on his forehead. "It is supposed to be a secret."

"What happens when you press the stone?" Could this be the way to Alexander's tomb? "Show me. One false move and you'll get my knife in your back."

They stepped inside and the priest pointed to a pair of blocks, each of which stuck out a fraction of an inch. "The bottom stone closes the door. The top one is the one I am supposed to press."

"What does it do?"

The priest shrugged.

"Oh, screw it." Lark placed her hand on the stone and pushed.

"Sorry," Spenser said, giving Maddock's hand a squeeze. "I really thought the eye would be here."

"Thanks, but what I mean is, this is not Alexander and this," he made a sweeping gesture, "is not Alexander's tomb."

"Maddock, I know you're disappointed and feel like you let us all down, and that's true, in a way," Grizzly said. "But it's not that big of a deal. Almost all of my discoveries are underwhelming."

"Hear me out. First of all, the body is too tall and lean to be Alexander. Second, look at the chest." He pointed to the exposed, leathery flesh, stretched out over the torso like a snare drum." Alexander suffered numerous injuries in battle and had several known and obvious scars. This flesh is smooth."

"I'm listening," Bones said tentatively.

"Alexander considered himself a god, an incarnation of the Egyptian God Amun. Where is the Egyptian symbology? Where are his own symbols, the lion, the bull, and the peacock? This place looks like a tourist trap made to fool gullible visitors."

"Or cocky Roman emperors." Bones scratched his chin, looked around. "Okay, smart guy. Where is the real tomb?"

Maddock frowned, glanced down at his feet, thinking hard. The sunburst image had been the key. And then he saw it.

"I think I've..."

"Do you guys hear something?" Bones asked. A moment later, a previously unseen door slammed shut, trapping them inside the chamber.

"Uh oh," Bones said.

From the corner of his eye, Maddock saw holes appear in the wall.

"Everybody down!" Maddock shouted. They hit the deck as darts buzzed through the air a few inches above the glass casket. A few seconds later another volley flew from the other direction.

"We're trapped in here," Spenser said. "What do we do?"

22

They hunkered down in the shelter of the steps that led up to the casket. Flying projectiles buzzed overhead.

"I'll bet that's only one of several booby traps," Bones said. "Any ideas?"

"A crazy one," Maddock said. "If we can rotate the second level of steps a quarter turn, it will form Alexander's sunburst pattern."

"Rotate it how?" Grizzly asked.

"Brute force I suppose. Hurry."

They got into position and began to push against the second step. Slowly, it gave way rotating on an invisible axis. They strained, muscles burned. All the while, darts intermittently flew through the air.

"I did not expect it to work," Bones said. "How did you know?"

"The shape, the distinctive pattern carved into the surface. Also, I noticed there's a tiny gap between the two levels."

"Very observant," Bones said. "Didn't think you had it in you."

When they had rotated the level a quarter of a turn, it suddenly stopped with a sharp clack. The top level, its points now evenly spaced between those of the bottom level, began to sink, taking the coffin with it.

"It really does resemble the Macedonian star pattern," Spenser said. "What happens now?"

With a rumbling sound, a door set in the far wall began to rise. They made a run for it, ducking and dodging the flying darts. They were halfway there when the a dull thud echoed through the chamber and the door slowly fell.

"Hurry!" Maddock shouted. One by one, they hurtled through the doorway. Maddock watched the ever-shrinking opening as the massive stone door fell like a guillotine blade. He dove forward, rolled, and made it through just as the door slammed shut.

After a pause to catch their breath, they moved down a wide, gently sloping passage made of stone blocks fitted together with remarkable precision. Where the passageway leveled out, dank water oozed from cracks, ran in rivulets down the slope, and pooled at the feet of a golden lion statue. The magnificent beast guarded an open doorway.

"This has got to be it," Bones said. "And I'll go first since you got it wrong last time."

"I wasn't exactly wrong," Maddock argued, but Bones wasn't listening. He was already on his way into the tomb. "Careful," Maddock said.

"You guys have got to see this!" Bones said.

They entered a small chamber. The floor was black marble, and the walls were lined with gold—real gold this time. Mosaics of precious gemstones covered three walls, forming a peacock, a lion, and a bull. There were gaps in the images where jewels had been removed. Bare sections of wall marked spots where the gold plating was stripped away.

"Cleopatra took gold and treasure from Alexander's tomb to finance Egypt's war with Rome," Maddock said. "This must be where she got it."

"Sure, blame it on the woman," Spenser chided. "I'm sure Antony had nothing to do with it."

In the next chamber, gilded statues of Zeus and Ammon, the gods of whom Alexander claimed to be the incarnation, barred their way. Behind them stood a row of statuary, all artistic masterpieces taken from the many lands Alexander had conquered. Wooden chests were stacked against the walls of the third chamber of the tomb. A few were intact, but many had broken apart, spilling coins, gems, artifacts, and ornate weapons. Others sat empty.

They passed through a narrow corridor and came face to face with a golden sphinx which guarded a rectangular pool of water, its surface filmy, its depths dark as night.

"Where's Alexander?" Grizzly said quietly.

"A pool of water had several meanings to the ancient Egyptians, including the afterlife, and the emergence of the Sun God into this world. Alexander was worshiped as a god. I think this pool is the passageway from Alexander's mortal life to the afterlife."

Spenser heaved a tired sigh. "I know appearance isn't everything, but I put a lot of work into my hair. You have no idea."

"I'll check it out first," Bones said. "Make sure Maddock isn't wrong again." He turned and plunged into the water. They watched as the light from his flashlight disappeared.

The seconds passed with agonizing slowness. Maddock waited, every muscle tense. Finally, the light reemerged, and then Bones head broke the surface.

"There's something on the other side. It's no more than ten meters, but there's a lot of debris in the water. Easy to get tangled."

"Which is why we swim with a buddy," Maddock said.

"Sorry, Dad. Won't happen again unless I feel like it."

Maddock and Spenser went first, while Bones and Grizzly brought up the rear. The cold, brackish water burned Maddock's eyes.

The floor of the pool was covered in silt and debris. As they swam the mount of refuse grew taller until it nearly reached the ceiling of the submerged corridor, leaving little room to swim past it.

Spenser suddenly jerked, let out a stream of bubbles. Had she been hurt? Caught in a trap? But then she turned and held up a human skull.

Maddock took a second look at the silt-covered debris. He saw more skulls, rib cages, femurs, and a single, skeletal hand reaching up out of the mire. These must be the remains of the slaves who had built the tomb.

When they reached the other side, Maddock caught a glimpse of a passageway off to his left that had once been blocked by an iron grate. The metal had rusted away. A few fish swam in and out. Did this passage reach the bay? There might be time later to check.

He swam to the surface and climbed out onto a ledge. Before them stood a golden door. A single word in ancient Greek was emblazoned on its surface.

Ἀλέξανδρος

"Does that say what I hope it says?" Spenser asked.

"Alexandros," Maddock said. "Or, as we know him, Alexander."

"We should wait for Bones and Grizzly." There was a note of doubt in Spenser's voice. "Weren't they right behind us?"

Maddock frowned. She was correct. Bones and Grizzly should be emerging from the depths any second. He waited but saw no sign of them.

"I'm going to check on them." He jumped in feetfirst and returned the way he had come. He saw movement, a flash of light, and swam for it.

Grizzly had gone limp. Bones was trying to pull him along, but their friend appeared to be stuck on something. Maddock reached their side and saw that Grizzly's boot was caught on a protruding humerus bone. He worked it free and helped Bones carry their friend to the surface.

"He's not breathing." Bones pressed his fingers to Grizzly's carotid artery. "If there's a pulse, I can't feel it."

Maddock wasted no time. He checked to see that

Grizzly's airway was clear, then began performing chest compressions. After thirty compressions, he added two rescue breaths. He was beginning the third set of rescue breaths when Grizzly began to cough. They rolled him onto his side, and he spat out a mouthful of water.

"I'm not dead?" he grunted.

"Only your brain," Bones said. "But that's always been the case."

Grizzly took a few seconds to catch his breath, then wobbled to his feet. Despite Spenser's protests, he insisted he was all right.

"This is not the first time I've drowned. I bounce back fast."

"Maybe swimming isn't your thing?" Bones suggested.

"My foot got stuck and I couldn't get loose. I tried to free it and banged my head on the ceiling. Next thing I knew, Spenser was kissing me."

"That was Maddock," Bones said. "He's been dying to lock lips with you since we met."

"It was rescue breathing," Maddock added.

"You couldn't do the chest compressions and let her do the mouth stuff?" Grizzly frowned, then broke into a smile. "I'm kidding. Thanks for saving my ass."

"Don't mention it," Maddock said.

"So, what's behind the door?" Grizzly's upbeat tone stood in stark contrast to his thin voice and wobbly legs.

"We're about to find out." Maddock took a breath, placed his hand on the door, and pushed.

The door swung open to reveal a pyramidal chamber. Shiny white marble streaked with veins of gold covered the walls and floor. A black marble vault stood at the center of the chamber, directly beneath the apex of the pyramid. Friezes depicting scenes from the life of Alexander adorned the sides.

Maddock and Bones exchanged glances. No words

were needed. While Spenser captured it on video, he and Bones took hold of the heavy lid and shifted it to the side. Bones shone his light inside.

"Holy crap," Bones said. "I don't believe it."

23

Maddock and Bones could only stare into the ancient sarcophagus. There was no golden casket inside, nor was there the body of Alexander. It held only a single stone box.

"What do you see?" Spenser asked. She approached slowly, camera focused on the open sarcophagus. When she could see inside, she frowned. "I don't understand. What is that?"

"An ossuary. It's a box used for storing human skeletal remains," Maddock said.

"Could those be Alexander's bones?" she asked, a note of doubt in her voice.

"It's not consistent with any account I've ever read," Maddock said. "Most witnesses said his body was remarkably well preserved. In some later accounts, he's a desiccated mummy. But all of them agree that his remains were intact."

"Who is it, then?" she asked.

"Only one way to find out." Bones reached in and removed the lid from the ossuary.

Inside were charred bones. Some showed cut marks, others had been smashed. The skull was missing. Maddock looked at Bones, who nodded, flashed a grin.

"You know what this means?" Bones asked.

"I believe I do."

"Would you care to fill us in?" Spenser asked as she zoomed in on the burned remains. "Unless this is Joan of Arc, I can't hazard a guess."

"I think this is Saint Mark."

"How? Isn't he buried in his tomb?" Grizzly asked.

"It's a long story," Maddock said. "Two years after Alexander's tomb disappeared from the historical record, ancient sources began referencing the tomb of Saint Mark in Alexandria. There had been no mention of it before, despite Mark having been dead for three hundred fifty years."

Bones took up the narrative. "The people of Alexandria got tired of Mark preaching what they saw as heresy against their gods. They tied a rope around his neck and dragged him through the city until he was decapitated. His body was burned but believers recovered his head. That continued to be the official story until the end of the fourth century. Around the same time as Saint Mark's tomb suddenly appeared in the historical record, so did a book called *The Acts of Saint Mark*. The writer claimed that God sent a storm to extinguish the flames, and Mark's body was recovered by believers."

"But how did his body..." Spenser began.

"Chill out. I'm getting there," Bones went on. "By the late seventh century, Muslims had conquered much of North Africa, including Alexandria. According to legend, Christians smuggled Mark's casket out of the city hidden under a wagonload of pork, knowing the Muslims wouldn't dig around inside. They loaded it onto a boat, and shipped it off to Italy. His remains ended up in a temporary tomb there until a cathedral was built to house it."

"Funny thing, people who handled the casket said it smelled of spices, like those used in mummification," Maddock added. "Christians at that time hated Pagans and despised their rituals. No way in hell would a Christian, especially one of Saint Mark's standing and renown, have been mummified."

"You think it was Alexander's body that was smuggled out, and Saint Mark's bones hidden down here?" Spenser said.

"And a fake Alexander was placed in a false tomb in case anyone went looking," Grizzly concluded. "It's a great story but how likely is it?"

"There are a few clues," Maddock said. "Mark's alleged temporary tomb in Italy included a relief carving of a Macedonian-style spear and the Star of Macedon, Alexander's symbol. Also, one witness reported honey leaking out of the casket. Some legends claim Alexander's body was preserved in honey."

"Why hasn't it been found already?" Spenser asked.

"It's an obscure legend. And the accepted story of Saint Mark's body is so pervasive that no one questions it. But this," he pointed to the ossuary, "proves that the body inside the casket could not have been that of Mark."

"I think we know where that body is now." Grizzly beamed, clapped his hands. "But how do we get out of here? We're locked in."

"I think I might have found a backdoor," Maddock said. "Are you up to another swim?"

"I'm ready."

They returned to the pool, but this time they swam through the low tunnel beyond the rusted gate. It was slow going against the current, and Maddock wondered if they would be forced to turn back, but the glow of sunlight danced just ahead.

The passageway made a sharp turn upward. They swam hard, passed through a pile of boulders, and emerged into open water.

Maddock had only a moment to suck in a breath of precious air before someone behind him shouted.

"Look out!"

He turned to see a tour boat bearing down on them. The man at the helm spotted the four swimmers and swerved, just missing them.

"Where are we?" Spenser gasped.

Maddock spotted a large stone fortress that resembled a medieval castle.

"The Qaitbay Citadel," he said. A fortress built on the

site where the Pharos Lighthouse once stood."

The tour boat circled around and returned to pick them up. Confused passengers helped them out of the water and onto the boat, where an angry sailor awaited them.

"What are you doing in the water?" he demanded, eying their sodden clothing.

"Abducted by a UFO," Bones said. "It dropped us here." He frowned, feigned confusion. "This is Miami, isn't it?"

The man frowned, shook his head.

"It's hard to explain," Maddock said. We're happy to pay you for a ride back to shore." He took out his waterproof wallet, essential in his line of work, and counted out several bills.

"I should report this to the authorities." He cast a meaningful glance at the wallet.

Maddock grimaced and handed him all the cash he had. That seemed to satisfy their rescuer.

"Enjoy your ride."

The passengers continued to stare at them. Their appearance was apparently more interesting than what they had seen on their tour. And then, an attractive blonde broke through the crowd and hurried over to them. It was Carly.

"Bones! Are you okay?" She wrapped her arms around the big man and squeezed him tight, oblivious to his wet clothes. "I'm so sorry I yelled at you. Forgive me?"

"Seriously?" Spenser muttered. "Has she ever heard of self-respect?

"Bones has a type," Maddock said. "I can't explain it."

"Just know that I will never be that forgiving."

Maddock chuckled. And then he heard what Carly was saying.

"Did your friends find you? The purple-haired woman and the surly redhead? They went into the church looking for you."

"How did they know we were here?" Bones asked.

"One of them follows Spenser on social media. We tagged her when we posted the pics we took with her. I hope that's not a problem?" Carly said.

"It's fine," Maddock assured her.

"What next?" Grizzly asked quietly.

"Now," Maddock said, "it's on to Italy!"

24

Jade put down the magnifying glass and rubbed her tired eyes. Since Maddock had dumped the astonishing artifact in her lap and bolted off, she had done little else but work on the translation. She was exhausted, but the work captivated her.

"It's past lunchtime. You should eat," Professor called from the kitchen.

"Seriously?" Jade looked around, taken aback by the bright sunlight, then glanced at her watch. One o'clock in the afternoon. "I just lost about five hours."

"Must be interesting reading."

"It is, as you would know if you were helping me translate," Jade muttered.

"That is true," Professor said as he slathered a bagel with peanut butter. "But somebody fired me." He paused, made a show of thinking hard. "I believe you said, '*Prof, you are too damn slow, and you move your lips when you read. Why don't you focus on something you're actually good at?*'"

"Let me guess. You're annoyed because I ended the sentence with a preposition?"

Professor chuckled. "It's always amusing when lesser primates demonstrate a primitive sense of humor." He plopped a bagel with peanut butter and sliced banana and a glass of milk down on the table in front of her. "Feeding time at the zoo. I don't know how you can stand that. It's like something Bones would eat."

"He calls it the Elvis," Jade said. "He also deep-fries his sandwiches like Elvis did, but that's a step too far for me."

"I thought you two disliked one another." Professor took the seat opposite her and took a swallow of coffee.

"Depends on the day. But I have to admit you and

Maddock are right. He's not entirely useless."

"Cheers." Professor raised his mug, and she clinked her glass of milk against it. He suddenly frowned. "Didn't you have lectures today?"

"Only one. I passed it off on Kaiana."

"The librarian who has a thing for you?" Professor frowned.

"It's a small college and she knows the material."

"What's the subject matter?"

"The cultural history of the Indus Valley region." A jolt of surprise hit her like an electric shock.

"What is it?" Professor sat up straight, a look of concern on his face.

"I just remembered something. According to what I just translated, Alexander found a sacred spring that had some healing properties. He believed the pool's ultimate source was in Eden. He suspected that the natives of the area knew the way. First, he tried to bribe the secret out of them, then he resorted to torture. In the end, he failed."

"Failed to extract the information?" Professor asked.

"Ptolemy is ambiguous. He says Alexander failed, but the elders told him of another path to Eden." Jade tugged at her ponytail, thinking hard. "That suggests there was, in fact, a gateway to Eden at this location."

"What if it's the Cities of Gold all over again?" Professor asked. "The natives fabricate stories of fabulous treasures that are just beyond the horizon. Anything to get the invaders to move along and leave them in peace."

"Didn't I tell you?" Jade said. "Maddock, Bones, and I solved that one years ago. In fact, that's how Maddock and I met." She grinned at Professor's dumbfounded expression. "Back to the subject at hand. The college has in its collection a map, drawn by Kamehameha, showing a small section of the Indus Valley region. Kaiana was thrilled when she stumbled across it. For some reason, she's an Indus Valley nerd."

"You think the sacred spring might be noted on the map?"

"Maybe. The spring was located near the place where Alexander's most steadfast companion fell."

"Hephaestion?" Professor asked.

"Wrong part of the world. Hephaestion died in what is now Iraq. And Alexander always referred to him in more intimate terms, like 'dearest' and 'beloved'. This was a different type of companion altogether, one whose loss was nearly as devastating as that of Hephaestion."

Professor squinted, thinking hard. His face split into a grin. "Bucephalus!"

Jade nodded. Bucephalus was Alexander the Great's warhorse. A powerful steed, he came into Alexander's possession when the teenage Alexander proved to be the only man who could tame the mighty stallion. Bucephalus remained Alexander's most faithful steed until he was killed after the Battle of the Hydaspes in 326 BC. A grieving Alexander buried his horse with honors and founded a city, Alexander Bucephalon, on the site. In time, the burial site was lost, with multiple locations in the Punjab region of southern Pakistan claiming the honor.

"Kamehameha was obviously on the same trail as Alexander. It stands to reason a hand-drawn map of a region where something so important to Alexander took place might contain pertinent information."

"Won't hurt to check," Professor said.

Jade picked up her phone and tapped Kaiana's contact information.

Kaiana was staring at her office wall when her phone rang. It was Jade. She closed her eyes, took a deep breath.

"Calm down, Kaiana," she said to herself. "Everything between the two of you is normal. She has no idea what you've gotten yourself into." Steeling herself, she accepted the call.

"Jade, how are you feeling?" she said brightly.

"Like crap. How did the lecture go?"

"Okay. I think I bored them to death."

"We're teachers, not performers. We inform, not entertain," Jade said.

"Okay, boomer."

Jade didn't laugh. "I could use your help with a project I'm working on."

Kaiana's heart skipped a beat. "What is it?"

"Do you remember showing me a map that belonged to Kamehameha? It was hand-drawn, showed an area on the outskirts of the Indus Valley?"

"Yes," Kaiana said weakly. Her mouth was dry, her palms suddenly sweaty. "It was part of the Indus Valley collection, which is how I stumbled across it."

"Do you think you could locate it for me?"

"No," Kaiana said sharply. "I mean, I can't put my hands on it right away. I think it might have been loaned out." It was a lie. She had seen to it that the map was in a safe place.

"To who?" Jade asked sharply. In the background, a man said, 'W*hom*'. Jade replied with a curse.

"I'll have to check," Kaiana said. "Is there anything specific you're looking for?"

"I would know it if I saw it," Jade said. "Any chance you have a digital image?"

"I do. I'll email it to you. It's a large file so it might take a few minutes." Her heart was pounding, and cold sweat dripped down the back of her neck. Might this be the breakthrough she had been hoping for?

Jade thanked her and hung up the phone. Hastily, Kainai called up the image on her hard drive. She had overheard enough of the conversation in Jade's office to know this had something to do with Alexander the Great. She zoomed in and scanned the image for anything that might be a clue. And then she saw it, an image like a watermark, so tiny and faint it was almost impossible to see. Eight points formed a Macedonian Star. She smiled, her tension eased a bit. This was exactly what she needed.

Hastily, she made a copy of the map, then opened up the copy in her graphics program. She zoomed in on the tiny image and began to blot it out. She was sort of an expert at Photoshop, but not in the Steve Carell way. A few pixels at a time, she covered up the sunburst. When she was satisfied, she emailed the altered copy to Jade.

Now, the moment had come. With trembling fingers, she dialed a number she had been forced to memorize.

"I have something you want," she said.

"This had better not be a waste of my time," Lark said. "I've had a disappointing day." She mumbled something about a tomb and a missing eye. Her harsh tone gave Kaiana the chills.

"It's a hand-drawn map belonging to Kamehameha. Jade Ihara just called asking for it. I checked and there's a very interesting symbol drawn so small and so faintly it almost escaped my notice."

"What sort of symbol?" Lark demanded.

"An eight-pointed star," she said casually.

"I want to see it." Lark sounded eager, almost hungry.

"Sorry to hear that," Kaiana said dully. "Send it to me now."

"I want my brother." Kaiana tried to sound firm, but Lark terrified her.

"Ah, Koa. Why are you worried about him?"

"I haven't heard from him in days. I want to see him, to know he's alive."

"Of course he's alive. We're at a highly sensitive place in our project." Lark paused. "Send me a copy of the map. If it is what you say it is, I will have you taken to him."

"Not good enough. I want him to come to me."

"Impossible. He's on the job and we can't spare him. I will have you flown to Lanai to see him. I'll even spring for a suite at a fancy hotel while you're there."

"All right," Kaiana reluctantly agreed. "Sending now." They remained on the line while Kaiana sent the file and told Lark exactly where to look.

"Excellent," Lark finally said. "I will send someone around to your house to collect you within the hour."

Kaiana rushed home, relieved to have finally given Lark what she wanted and eager to see her brother again. Perhaps they could finally be free of the strange woman and her organization.

When she entered her apartment, she was surprised to see a woman sitting on the sofa. She was solidly built, her chestnut hair graying at the temples.

"Who are you?" Kaiana asked.

"I'm Phyllis. Lark sent me."

"Usually, visitors wait to be let in," Kaiana said. "I'll just need a minute to pack a bag."

"That won't be necessary, sweetie," Phyllis said.

"What are you talking about? I'm supposed to see my brother."

Phyllis drew a pistol and aimed it at Kaiana.

"You'll be joining your brother shortly."

25

The Basilica di San Marco stood at the end of the famed Saint Mark's Square. The square had once been the political and religious center of the Republic of Venice, but now it was home to cafes and restaurants.

Maddock and Spenser strolled across the moonlit square, admiring the sights. An astrological clock tower, a spectacular bell tower, and the Doge's Palace dominated the square. A breeze blew in off the canal, carrying with it the faint aroma of garlic from the few cafes and restaurants which remained open at this late hour.

"I always heard the canals stink, but it doesn't seem to be true," Spenser said, snapping photos as she walked.

"That was true fifty years ago, but no longer," Maddock said. "The city cleaned things up a long time ago."

They reached their destination and paused to admire it. The basilica was the episcopal seat of the Patriarch of Venice. Blending the architectural styles of East and West, the spectacular basilica had been constructed specifically to house the alleged remains of Saint Mark.

"It's beautiful," Spenser marveled as she gazed at the famous cathedral.

It was a magnificent sight. Five recessed portals which alternated with large piers comprised the lower register. Elaborate Gothic crowning adorned the upper register. A series of arches were decorated with foliage and topped by statues of saints. At the center stood a statue of Saint Mark, flanked by angels on either side.

"It's about time," a voice called out. Bones sat on a wall nearby, drinking a glass of beer. Grizzly stood a short distance away, speaking with an olive-skinned woman of middle years.

"We're five minutes early," Spenser said.

"Five minutes early is ten minutes late," Bones replied. He chugged the rest of his drink, tossed the glass into a garbage bin, and let out a loud belch that reverberated through the empty square.

"Nice." Spenser rolled her eyes.

Grizzly introduced them to Ornella, their guide. She was an attractive woman with slight tilted brown eyes, chestnut hair, and a perpetual sneer. She was an actress with whom Grizzly had worked years ago. From the tenor of the conversation, Maddock got the impression that her career had taken a steep downturn.

"Ornella works part-time as a tour guide," Grizzly explained. "Rather, she did until recently." He cleared his throat. "There was an issue involving a handsy. He didn't appreciate the way she defended herself."

"Good for you," Spenser said.

"*Bastardi*! All of them," Ornella swore.

"Anyway, she still has access to the cathedral, and she has agreed to help us."

"We should go now," Ornella said. "We don't want to be seen lurking around here when no night tours are scheduled. Come."

She led them around the basilica and down to a footbridge that spanned the Rio del Palazzo, one of the many canals that wound through the city.

"We must swim," Ornella said.

"I thought you had access to the basilica," Grizzly said.

"I told you I know how to get inside without being spotted by security cameras," she said.

Spenser let out a low groan, absently ran a hand through her hair. "Story of my life," she said. "Let's get this over with."

One by one, they vaulted the bridge rail and dropped down into the water. A short swim underwater led to an opening in the stone wall of the canal. They passed through an old storm drain until they reached a vertical shaft. They swam to the top and emerged in a forgotten crawlspace.

"Where are we?" Spenser asked.

"Underneath the Chiesa di San Teodoro. It is a church that sits beside the Basilica. Much less famous, much less secure."

They made their way on hands and knees across the room and squeezed through a crack in the foundation, then entered another damp, dark space. The smell of mildew hung heavy in the air. They skirted pools of stagnant water and came to a pile of stones.

"A little help?" Ornella asked as she began moving rocks. Bones was only too happy to assist an attractive woman. Together they moved rocks aside to reveal an iron grate set in the wall. "It is not bolted in. A little secret." She tapped her nose and winked at Bones, who grinned back.

Bones removed the grate and set it aside. Through the opening, they saw a vaulted ceiling of stone blocks supported by ornate marble columns. They climbed through and found themselves standing inside a crypt. Security lights cast a faint blue glow on the tiled floor.

"This is the crypt underneath the basilica," Ornella said. "Saint Mark's body was once entombed down here but was moved up to the chancel because of flooding."

Their footsteps echoed through the empty crypt as they followed Ornella up into the chancel. Maddock caught himself holding his breath as they approached the altar. The church was a spectacular sight. The interior of the domes, the vaults, and the upper walls were adorned with gold-ground mosaics depicting saints, prophets, and scenes from the Bible. When they reached the altar, they paused and stared.

The sarcophagus of Saint Mark lay beneath a heavy marble altar. Inscribed on it were four words:

CORPVS DI SAN MARCO

"The body of Saint Mark." Ornella's voice held a note of reverence.

"I thought you hated this place," Bones said.

She gave her head a quick shake. "I love the church. But there is one priest I hate very much." She lapsed into contemplative silence.

Maddock made a slow circuit around the altar, scrutinizing every inch. When he finished, he took a step back, scratched his chin. Something was not right. He had seen photographs but had expected it to be larger. When he took into account the apparent thickness of the sides, he doubted it could hold the body of Alexander the Great, or anyone else for that matter.

"Seems a bit on the small side," Bones said. "Sort of like your…"

"We're inside a church, Bones," Spenser said.

"Planning to desecrate the final resting place of a saint," Bones replied.

"You are going to do what?" Ornella hissed.

"That's not what he means." Maddock looked around at the mosaics, thinking hard. He had an idea. He turned to Ornella.

"Have you ever seen a symbol like this one?" He showed her a photo of the Macedonian Star symbol that had been found somewhere in the crypt years ago.

Her eyes went wide, and she took a step back. She took a few deep breaths, then nodded. "There is a place that was closed off long ago. It was damaged by flooding and is said to be dangerous. No one is supposed to go there."

"But you have been there?" Maddock asked.

She grimaced, her face twisted into a nauseated expression. "I was tricked. A priest lured me there and attacked me." Tears welled in her eyes. "He got me to the ground, and I bit off his earlobe." She smiled at the memory.

"Yass, Queen!" Spenser said.

"That's why she lost her job as a guide," Grizzly said. "The priest told everyone it was she who attacked him."

"Of course they believed him." Spenser rolled her eyes.

"If it's not too difficult for you, would you show us the place?" Maddock asked.

Ornella hesitated, then nodded. She guided them through the crypt to a far corner where a tall iron gate barred their way. A sign written in English and Italian warned visitors against entry. The entire setup was intended to deter curious tourists, not to withstand any serious break-in attempt. Bones picked the lock in a matter of seconds.

They proceeded down a narrow corridor. The marble lining had fallen in places, exposing the bricks, some of them crumbling, that formed the walls. They stepped over a line of caution tape, rounded a corner, and found themselves standing in a small chamber with a low ceiling. Ornella moved to the far wall and ran her fingers over the bricks.

"The marking is faint. I only saw it for a moment when he shoved me against the wall." Her expression darkened, then brightened again. "Here it is!

»

26

Maddock could just make out the symbol. He brushed away a layer of grime and smiled. It was the Macedonian Star!

"Here goes nothing." Maddock pressed on the brick. It slid back, and then a previously unseen door swung open.

"Holy crap!" Bones said.

Beyond the door lay a large vault. At the center stood a large marble sarcophagus. Dust and grime coated its surface.

"What is this place?" Ornella said.

"Somewhere that hasn't been seen in a thousand years," Maddock said.

This is going to make terrific television." Grizzly turned to Spenser. "You are getting this?"

"Every second," she said, aiming her camera at the sarcophagus.

"You realize all you're doing is making a record of our crimes," Bones said.

"We have connections and good lawyers," Grizzly said. "It'll work out. Let's do this." With that, he turned to the camera and began improvising. "Folks, this is it! For the first time in nearly two-thousand years, mankind will gaze upon the face of Alexander the Great!"

"Humankind," Spenser corrected.

"We'll fix it in post." Grizzly proceeded to the sarcophagus and beckoned for Maddock and Bones to join him.

"Who put him in charge?" Bones asked.

"I think he cowboyed it," Maddock replied.

"To be fair, he is paying for everything," Spenser said.

"True. We'll let him think he's in charge... for now." Maddock chuckled as he and Bones followed their friend into the vault.

Maddock, Bones, and Grizzly carefully removed the lid and shined their lights inside. A golden glow shone all around as the beams danced on the surface of the honey-colored liquid that filled the sarcophagus. Beneath the surface of the liquid lay a man. All of them recognized his face.

"Alexander," Maddock said.

"Madre di Dio," Ornella whispered.

The great conqueror lay in silent repose. Remarkably, his body was perfectly preserved. He appeared as if he might wake at any second.

"He looks like he died yesterday," Grizzly said.

"What is this stuff?" Bones dipped into the golden liquid and rubbed it between his thumb and forefinger. "It's not sticky or viscous. It's almost like water."

Maddock didn't reply. His eyes were locked on what hung around Alexander's neck—a chain with an orb hanging from it.

"The Eye of Alexander," Maddock said.

Grizzly turned to the camera. "And this is what we have been looking for." With that, he plunged his hand into the sarcophagus, unhooked the chain, and held it up for all to see.

Where the stone Maddock had discovered in Kamehameha's tomb was amber, this one was topaz. It had the same golden iris and vertical pupil. Gold liquid dripped from it.

"Are you crazy?" Maddock said. "We don't know what this stuff is."

"Doesn't seem to be bothering me," Grizzly said, wiping the liquid onto his pants. "What do you know? The cut on my hand has healed. Excellent!"

Before they could examine the body further, they heard distant voices.

"I thought there were no tours tonight," Grizzly said to

Ornella.

"There aren't," she said, frowning.

"Let's close the sarcophagus and get the hell out of here," Maddock said. They hastily went about their business. Within a minute, they were on their way out. The secret vault was sealed again, and dirt smeared over the Macedonian Star symbol.

"Where are we going?" It was the voice of a young woman from somewhere close by.

"I am going to show you something special. Few have ever seen it."

Ornella hissed a curse. "That is the priest who tried to…" She couldn't finish the sentence.

"I've got this," Maddock said. He walked purposefully toward the sound of the voices.

Around the corner came a dark-haired man. He was tall, broad-shouldered, and muscular. Most of his right earlobe was missing. He halted when he saw Maddock striding in his direction.

"Who are you?" The priest demanded.

"I'm your penance."

Maddock drove his fist into the larger man's chin. The priest's eyes rolled back, and his legs gave out. He hit the ground and lay there unconscious. He turned to the young woman who stood gaping at him.

"Run." A former officer in the Navy, Maddock knew how to issue a command, and she responded to his tone immediately, turning and fleeing.

"Nice one," Bones said.

"Thanks. Now let's get the hell out of here."

27

Maddock awoke in the middle of the night to the sound of his phone vibrating. He rolled over, rubbed his eyes, and looked at the screen. It was Jade.

"What's up?" he replied drowsily.

"What's up? Your telephone etiquette needs work," Jade said.

"It's three in the morning," he grumbled.

"We finished translating the scroll, but I guess you're too sleepy to hear what it says."

Maddock sat upright, suddenly wide awake. Beside him, Spenser rolled over and cast a questioning look at him.

"Who is it?" she mumbled.

"Jade has translated the scroll. Get Bones and Grizzly."

Spenser knocked on the inside door that connected to the adjacent hotel room. Bones and Grizzly meandered in, rubbing sleep from their eyes.

"I can't believe you made me room with him." Bones pointed with his thumb at Grizzly. "Dude snores to wake the dead."

"Complain later," Maddock said. "Jade has news." He turned on the speakerphone and they listened as Jade summarized what she had translated.

The scroll, a previously unknown chapter of Ptolemy's book, told the story of Adam's search for the land of Eden. Upon conquering Babylon, Alexander discovered ancient fragments of text that predated even the Epic of Gilgamesh. He learned of the keys to Eden, a pair of gemstones that resembled eyes. These stones had belonged to Lilith, Adam's first wife, and she promised to grant the treasure of Eden to the one who returned them.

Alexander found the eyes and eventually discovered a

sacred spring in the Indus Valley region that he believed was linked to Eden. After failing to find a way into the fabled land, he extracted information from the elders that led him to a gateway.

"He crossed Adam's Bridge and climbed the sacred mountain where the First Man entered the world. There he found a temple and beneath it, a doorway to Eden," Jade read.

"Adam's Bridge," Maddock said. "That rings a bell."

"I'll tell you all about it in a minute," Jade said. "Now, shut up. I'm nearly finished."

"She's been in a mood all day," Professor said in the background.

"You can shut up, too," Jade said. She quickly summarized the remainder of the text.

Alexander took eleven men into Eden. They followed a pathway into the valley of the monkey men, who guided them through the swampy land of the serpents. But when they reached the home of Lilith, they were forced to turn back.

"Alexander returned alone, shaken to his core, and vowed never to return to Eden," Jade finished.

"Any idea what forced him to turn back?" Bones asked.

"None," Jade said.

"Anyone know what Adam's Bridge is, or the sacred mountain?"

"Adam's Bridge, also known as Rama Setu, was a land bridge that once connected Sri Lanka with the southern tip of India. It was above water until about eight hundred years ago," Jade said.

"Was it man-made?" Bones asked.

"According to Hindu legend, it was made by an army of monkey men," Jade said.

"Coincidence?" Bones said. "I think not."

"What about the sacred mountain?" Spenser asked.

"Adam's Peak!" Maddock said. "It's a mountain in central Sri Lanka. There's a giant footprint in the stone that is said to have been made by Adam, as well as an ancient temple."

"I remember now," Bones said. "There are all sorts of open spaces beneath the temple, but no one has ever been allowed to explore them."

"It's a place of religious significance for Christians, Buddhists, Hindus, and Muslim cultures," Jade said. "They're very protective of it."

"Think they would do it as a favor to a celebrity?" Grizzly asked.

"It's been tried," Jade said. "No cameras, no outsiders. I reached out to Tam Broderick to see if she could help."

"I wish you had talked to me first," Maddock said.

"Did you not promise to keep her in the loop?" Jade said.

"I did," Maddock admitted. "What did she say?"

"Tam says there are strange things afoot there. Magnetic anomalies, all sorts. At one time the intelligence community was concerned the temple might be a cover for the development of an advanced weapon of some sort, but they concluded it's a naturally occurring phenomenon."

"The data is fascinating," Professor said. "The phenomenon is not unique to Adam's Peak. Similar readings have been found in several places, including southern Pakistan in the area where Alexander discovered the sacred spring, in Arabia, which Alexander was planning to invade, and beneath the Red Sea."

"I knew it!" Maddock said.

"I think these places are akin to wormholes," Professor continued. The science isn't easy to distill, but suffice it to say, two distant places are connected by cosmic strings. If you can make the energy field on one end of the cosmic string match the other, a pathway is opened between the two."

"How do we create those conditions?" Maddock asked.

"I have a theory. Turn on your television and hold the eye close to the screen."

Maddock did as Professor said. When he held the eye close to the television, a circle appeared in the middle of the screen, a spinning vortex of static, that followed the eye as it swung back and forth.

"The eyes must emit a signal which creates the perfect conditions to open the wormhole."

"That's great," Bones said. "Can Tam get us inside?"

"She says the place is run by a group who claims to protect our world from the underworld. The only way someone can visit the lowest levels of the temple is to be escorted there by an initiate."

"Does this group have a name?" Spenser asked eagerly. She looked at Maddock. He could tell they were thinking the same thing.

"It varies. In America, they are called Guardians."

Maddock laughed and Spenser clapped her hands. They exchanged an enthusiastic high-five.

"I take it this is good news?" Jade asked.

"We happen to know two guardians," Maddock said, "and they owe us a big favor."

28

Adam's Peak was a conical mountain standing over seven thousand feet tall. Located in central Sri Lanka, it was best known for the Sri Pada, or "sacred footprint," a foot-shaped rock formation near the summit. Depending on the legend, it was considered to be the footprint of Buddha, Shiva, St. Thomas, or Adam.

"Not very impressive," Spenser said, looking down at the print. "It looks like a blob, not a footprint."

"You get grumpy when you're tired," Bones said.

The climb had taken four exhausting hours. Now they stood atop the famed peak, looking out at the jungle below. Most tourists climbed the peak in order to watch the sun rise. Maddock and his friends were here on more pressing business.

As they made their way through the throngs of tourists, many stopped to gawk at Bones. A Native American was an uncommon sight, here, but one of Bones' height and breadth of shoulder was a rarity anywhere. A couple of them recognized Grizzly, who was all too eager to pose for photographs.

"Good thing there's no signal up here," Maddock said to Bones. "Between the television presenter, the social media star, and your ugly ass, we can't go anywhere without someone noticing."

"You're just mad that no one cares who you are," Bones said.

Maddock shook his head and led the way to the Buddhist temple that stood at the center of the several buildings that surmounted the peak. A man in red robes greeted them. He frowned when Maddock introduced himself but motioned for them to enter. He guided them through the main floor, adorned with red and gold tapestries, and down into the lower levels.

Three elders, two men and a woman, sat on cushions in the middle of a small room. All had shaved heads and were clad in robes of snowy white. They watched in silence as Maddock and his friends took seats facing them.

The woman stood, looked at the guide, and inclined her head toward the door. The man hesitated, but when he saw her frown, he bowed himself out and closed the door behind him.

"You are the people Lou Deng spoke of." It was not a question.

"We are," Maddock replied. Lou Deng and his friend Chan were Guardians who lived in New York City and secretly protected its citizens from a creature called the Nian—a ferocious dragon-like creature with golden scales. Maddock and Spenser had recently aided the two men in fighting off the creature and returning it to its domain. Despite owing them a favor, Lou and Chan had needed some convincing before they agreed to intercede on Maddock's behalf. According to them, the temple at Adam's Peak was a place best avoided.

The woman introduced herself as Butiwati. Her stony-faced companions were called Baskoro and Candra. Maddock in turn introduced himself and his friends.

"Bones and Grizzly?" Butiwati asked.

"Uriah and Donald are their birth names, but they prefer their nicknames."

"I understand. We abandoned our original names when we gave our lives to the temple and its mission." She looked them up and down, taking their measure. "Tell me why you wish to pass through the door."

"So there really is a door?" Grizzly asked. "Sorry," he added when the three elders turned their icy gaze upon him.

"We are all in danger. Several attempts on our lives

have been made. They have murdered at least two people in an effort to cover up their crimes."

"You have a key?"

Maddock took out the stone and held it aloft. The three elders leaned forward, fascinated.

"Where did you get it?" Baskoro asked. His voice was surprisingly deep.

Maddock saw no point in lying. "From the tomb of Alexander the Great."

"We have heard no news of its discovery," Butiwati said.

"It remains a secret," Maddock said. "We only wanted the key."

The elders stood, moved out of earshot and began talking quietly. It soon became apparent that Baskoro was not on their side. They argued for several minutes before he appeared to relent.

"Come with us," Butiwati said.

She led them down a spiraling stone staircase. Water dripped from the walls and made the steps slick. They walked until Maddock could not guess how far they had gone. They finally reached the bottom and found themselves in a subterranean cavern, standing before a golden door. Upon it was engraved a large hand. Its skin was scaly like that of a reptile, the fingers tipped with sharp claws. An eye was carved in the middle of a palm. The circular indentation was exactly the size of the blue orb they had recovered from Alexander's tomb.

"No one has passed through this door since Alexander," Butiwati said. "It is said he entered brimming with confidence but returned a shadow of himself."

"Did he find treasure?" Bones asked.

"Would you consider a jar of bees and a honeycomb a treasure?"

Maddock exchanged glances with his companions.

Had they learned the source of the honey-like liquid that preserved Alexander's remains?

"Do you have any idea what's waiting on the other side?" Bones asked.

"You will find out soon enough. I will light candles for you and pray for your return." She bowed to each of them in turn, then took a step back and waited.

Spenser aimed her camera at the door and frowned. "It's not working."

"In that case, we might as well get on with it." Maddock fitted the stone into the eye socket on the door.

It flared up immediately, shining with brilliant light. The blue glow flowed out like water across the serpent's hand, outlining every detail. And then, the door swung open.

29

Maddock stepped through a curtain of mist and into another world. It was oppressively hot, the air moist. Even gravity felt stronger here, like a weight on his shoulders. Obscured by the haze, a circle of light high above shone down with a pale glow.

"It's like a greenhouse in here," Bones said, tugging at the neckline of his shirt.

"This is going to do wonders for my hair," Spenser said.

"Mine too," Grizzly said, running a hand through his wavy brown hair.

They stood on a narrow ledge on the side of a cliff. A steep path led down into the haze. No telling what lay ahead of them, but there was nowhere else to go.

Maddock looked back at the door through which they had come. For a moment he had feared it might vanish, but it was still there.

"The hand is different," Maddock said.

On this side of the door, the hand-carved into the surface was that of a human. No scales, no claws. Maddock frowned. If this symbol indicated that the world of humans lay on the other side, then what had he and the others walked into? He supposed they would find out soon enough.

They made the long journey down the cliff trail and entered a lush tropical jungle. Everything here looked dangerous. Thorny bushes, leaves with jagged edges, and Venus flytraps twelve feet tall. The ground was mushy and foul-smelling. Tree branches laden with bulbous green fruit, hung low overhead.

"Try not to touch anything," Maddock said to Bones.

"We should get some footage," Grizzly said. "I'll narrate. Let me know when you're ready. He nodded at

Spenser who raised her camera and immediately let out a curse.

"It's dead. I made sure it was fully charged." She took out her phone. "It's dead too. I wonder if passing over to another world caused them to short out?"

The others checked their electronic devices and discovered that theirs, too, were no longer operational.

"Flashlights don't work either," Grizzly reported.

Bones drew his pistol and took aim at one of the heavy fruits hanging above them.

"What are you doing?" Maddock said. "You'll draw attention to us."

"If my sidearm is going to fail on me, I want to know now." Bones squeezed the trigger. Nothing. He ejected the bullet and examined it. "Looks okay." He tried again with the same result.

"Maybe the laws of physics are somehow different here?" Grizzly offered.

"Looks like it." Bones holstered his weapon. "This could be a problem

---

The land of Eden was not what Isla had expected. It was sticky and foul-smelling. The damp earth squelched with every step. It was as if the entire world was ripening and rotting before her eyes.

"Why is it so hot here? I thought Eden was supposed to be a paradise." Lark had not stopped complaining since they had arrived.

"Will you stop your moaning?" Isla snapped. "You never know who or what is listening." She froze in her tracks as a huge snake, neon yellow with purple diamonds along its back, slithered across their path. It paid them no mind—probably a good thing as it was the size of a giant anaconda.

"Are all Scots as bitchy as you?" Lark grumbled.

"They are when saddled with a partner who is constantly whinging."

"She's angry because you killed that old man," Tama said.

"You didn't have to do that," Hunt added. His eyes were still black from Maddock bashing him in the head with a shovel, the bruises now a sickly purple and yellow.

The map Kaiana had provided them had led them to the remains of an ancient settlement. It had taken some enhanced interrogation techniques, but the villagers had finally confirmed the Alexander legend. A pair of them, twins who claimed to be nearly a hundred years old, had guided them into the depths of a mountain cave and shown them what remained of the sacred spring visited by Alexander so many years ago. It was now a tiny pool, fed by the occasional droplet of water.

Isla could still remember what it felt like when she dipped her finger into the pool. It was ice cold, and when she touched her wet finger to the tip of her tongue, she had experienced a moment of ecstasy that faded away all too quickly. That was when things turned ugly.

Initially, the old men denied knowledge of any sort of doorway. After more questioning, and the extraction of a few teeth, one had admitted to the existence of the doorway, but claimed that the passageway leading to it had collapsed long before the time of Alexander. That was when Lark had taken matters into her own hands. With his twin dead, the surviving man had shown them the way.

"I had to shoot him. They would never have shown us the way otherwise," Lark said.

"We would have found the door eventually," Hunt

complained.

"I think you just enjoy shooting people," Tama said.

"And don't you forget it." Lark winked at the big islander, who scowled and clenched his fists.

"This is why I hate working with men," Lark said. "They don't have the stomach to do what needs to be done.

Isla had not wanted to bring the two men along, but she was running out of agents. Two of them had gotten themselves arrested after driving off a cliff. The third was tying up loose ends in the Hawaiian Islands.

Isla knew there was no point in arguing with Lark. She was a true believer, someone so devoted to her cause that she rarely subjected her actions to any sort of critical thinking. She was like a pistol prone to misfiring—sometimes useful, but an ever-present danger.

They lapsed into silence as they trudged along, following a well-worn path down into a valley. In all of their research, they had not found any description of the land, much less a map. She had to hope that this path would lead to their destination.

Up ahead they heard a hissing sound. She froze, turned, and held a finger to her lips for silence. Quietly they crept forward.

Three figures, each carrying a spear, stood in the pathway. At first glance, they appeared to be human, but on closer inspection, Isla realized they were something else. They were tall, thin, and hairless. Their eyes were bright green, the pupils vertical slits. They had no noses, only nostrils.

"What in the hell are those things?" Lark whispered.

Isla silenced her with a glare. Lizard people were the stuff of ancient myth and modern conspiracy theories. But these were no myths.

As she watched, one of them turned, raised his head, and stuck out his forked tongue. He moved it from side to side a few times as if tasting the air. Suddenly, his eyes locked on the spot where Isla and her team hid. He hissed something that almost sounded like recognizable speech, and pointed directly at them. He and his companions hefted their spears and headed in Isla's direction.

Predictably, Lark stood, drew her weapon, and pulled the trigger. It made a clicking sound but did not fire. The lizardmen quickened their pace.

"Dammit! It's a dud," Lark swore.

Tama and Hunt drew their weapons but met with similar results. It seemed firearms did not work in this place. Primitive weapons, however, worked fine. The lizardmen proved that by hurling their spears at Isla and her party. She and Lark got out of the way. Tama and Hunt were too slow. Tama took a spear in the heart, Hunt in the belly.

To their right and left, rustling sounds filled the jungle. Isla caught a glimpse of more of the strange beings moving toward them.

"They're trying to surround us," she said.

"What do we do?" Lark asked.

"Run!"

30

Maddock had no idea how long they had been walking. Neither his watch nor his cellphone worked. What was more, the position of the sun never changed, meaning he could not use it to estimate the passage of time. All he knew for certain was they were all dripping wet from the heat. Spenser had traded her safari-style outfit for khaki shorts and a sports bra. It was a measure of their weariness that Bones didn't make a single inappropriate comment.

"Do you think we're going in the right direction?" Grizzly asked for the third time.

"We scouted around, and this was the only path. Remember?" Maddock said tightly. Grizzly didn't mean to be a pain in the ass; he simply loved to talk.

"I'll bet this is the same path Alexander walked," Grizzly said. "It's crazy to think about."

Maddock nodded. He was so focused on the fact they didn't know where they were going that he hadn't reflected on where they were. This was Eden! It wasn't what he had expected, but it was real.

"Anyone want an orange slice?" Spenser asked, deftly slicing through the peel with the tip of one long fingernail. "I've also got sunscreen and insect repellant if anyone needs it."

Bones frowned, tugged at his ponytail. "You know something? I haven't seen a single insect."

Maddock nodded. Bones was right. If they were back home in Florida, they would have been fighting off clouds of mosquitoes and swarming gnats. Here, there were none. Not that he was complaining.

Up ahead, the trees began to shake. A cloud of white burst forth and flew in all directions. Their wings made whistling sounds as they flapped.

"Are those birds?" Spenser asked nervously as several of the flying creatures winged in their direction.

"Nope," Bones said. "Those are hairless bats."

Maddock watched the bats zip toward them. As an experienced caver, he had no fear of bats. They were misunderstood creatures. Still, something was bothering him, but he couldn't put a finger on it. And then it came to him.

"If there are no insects, what do the bats eat?"

"Holy crap," Bones said. "Vampire bats!" He drew his knife as the bats dove down upon them. He swung but the attackers easily evaded his strike.

Spenser let out a cry and covered her head. Maddock tackled her out of the way, then turned to face the flying bloodsuckers. A cacophony of shrieks pierced his ears.

The bats were down on the path, fighting over the orange Spenser had dropped. Even as they fought, more bats cried out and began flying toward them.

"I forgot about fruit bats," Bones admitted.

"Still, I'd like to get out of their way," Maddock said.

They ran until they came to a stream. It was sluggish, the water murky. A pink tadpole as large as Maddock's fist swam past. A few seconds later, a thunderous croak filled the air.

"Did somebody strangle a hippo?" Bones asked, looking around.

"No, but I see a hippo-sized frog." Grizzly pointed downstream at a mottled shape that Maddock had thought to be a boulder.

It was a gigantic frog. It gazed at them through golden eyes the size of grapefruits.

"Glad it's a frog," Bones said, "and not something dangerous."

As if in response, the frog opened its mouth. Maddock

had a split second to react. "Get down!" he shouted.

Something like a pink rope shot through the air. It missed them by inches and slammed into the trunk of a tree, where it stuck.

"That's a big tongue!" Bones said.

"Shut up and run!" Maddock yelled.

They took off at a dead sprint. Behind them, the frog let out another croak that Maddock felt down to his fillings. He glanced back to see the tree come crashing down.

The path veered away from the river. It seemed the gigantic creature had no interest in leaving its watery domain. After a few minutes, they decided it was safe to slow down.

"This is a weird freaking place," Bones said.

"Wasn't Eden supposed to be a paradise?" Grizzly asked.

"Only the garden God made in Eden," Maddock said. "We don't know what the rest of the land was like."

Spenser looked around, grimaced. "I'm definitely leaving a negative review on TripAdvisor."

They walked along, catching their breath. As they moved deeper into the jungle, the air cooled a little and the light overhead began to dim. Still, it was hot.

"I hear something." Bones inclined his head, frowned, listening hard. "Sounds like somebody crying for help."

They took off at a fast trot. The soft earth dulled the sound of their footfalls as they ran. Now Maddock heard the sound—a high-pitched shriek.

"Sounds like a woman, I think." Spenser sounded uncertain.

"A banshee, maybe," Grizzly said.

Up ahead, the jungle thinned. Maddock saw the remnants of an old stone wall. It had collapsed in sections and the jungle had taken over. Carved into the surface of one of the intact sections was a spiral snake motif, a symbol common to ancient cultures around the world.

On the other side of the wall, a bizarre standoff was taking place. A small man in a brown suit was facing off against half-a-dozen taller men. In a millisecond he realized his initial assessment was incorrect. The mind had a way of trying to make sense of the bizarre by labeling it in a familiar way. But these were not men. At least, they were not human men.

The attackers were tall, skinny, bipedal creatures with reptilian eyes and flat noses. Their scaly skin ranged in color from an olive green that was almost black to a neon green worthy of a Myrtle Beach t-shirt shop. They all brandished bronze-tipped spears.

"What are those things?" Spenser said.

"I don't know, but they're definitely in Slytherin," Spenser said.

The lizardmen's intended victim was no more than five feet tall. He had a pale face with a protuberant snout like a chimpanzee. His body was covered in russet-colored fur. He was armed with a whip, which he used to keep the reptilian creatures at bay. He moved with remarkable agility but could not escape his attackers.

"The monkey men who built Adam's Bridge," Spenser said.

The small man spotted them. He blinked, dodged a spear thrust, and then cried out to them. Maddock did not know the words, but somehow, he heard them in his mind clear as day.

"Help me!"

Maddock could not leave the poor creature behind, nor did he relish the thought of having the scaled warriors dogging his trail once they finished the job here. Instinct told him they would have to face these creatures eventually. Might as well have the element of surprise on their side.

Bones seemed to feel it too. He ran shoulder-to-shoulder with Maddock. Grizzly and Spenser lagged a few steps behind.

Bones got there first. He crashed into one of the creatures and sent it flying into one of its companions. The pair tumbled to the ground and lay there stunned.

Another of the beasts turned around to face Maddock. It let out a hiss and Maddock punched it square in the nose. The creature dropped like a bag of wet cement.

"The nose is vulnerable!" he shouted, scooping up the spear the creature had dropped.

"Good to know," Spenser replied. One of the fallen creatures was up on all fours, struggling to regain its feet. She dashed up to it and kicked it in the face. The thing went lip, fell facedown in the soft earth. She let out a triumphant cheer, then gave its companion similar treatment.

"You are bloodthirsty!" Maddock called, dancing to the side and Grizzly and a lizardman rolled past him. Grizzly ended up on top and rained punches down on his adversary.

"I've been studying martial arts," she said.

"I didn't know that."

"I wanted it to be a surprise." She flashed a dazzling smile.

One lizardman remained standing. Bones had disarmed it. The two faced off, fists raised. Bones flicked a jab at the creature, and it sprang back, stumbled.

"Quit playing with your food," Maddock said.

"I wanted an assessment of its fighting skills." Bones dodged a swipe of the lizardman's clawed hand, and countered with a half-strength punch to the creature's chin. It stumbled backward toward Maddock, who pinned its arms. The creature thrashed around, but could not break free.

"Who are you?" Maddock demanded. The creature only hissed.

"The Naga will not answer your questions," the

monkey man said. "They have limited autonomy. The reptile brain, you know." He tapped his cranium. "It is what makes them such poor fighters. But there are many of them, and they are avaricious."

"I thought Naga were like the snake version of mermaids," Bones said. "Snake on the bottom, party up top?"

The monkey man blinked. "I do not understand your use of the word 'party.' But the Ninazu are as you describe."

"Ninazu?" Maddock echoed. Ninazu was the name of a Mesopotamian god of the underworld who was associated with snakes.

"They are the leaders among the Naga." The Naga hissed and once again tried to break free.

"What do you suggest we do with this thing?" Maddock asked.

The little man picked up a spear and ran the Naga through. He watched the creature's death throes with casual disinterest. When the Naga was dead, he turned back to Maddock and his companions.

"I am Maruti. I owe you a life debt." He made a little bow.

Maddock realized that, although he heard Maruti's words in English, he was speaking a different language entirely. His lip movements did not align with what Maddock was hearing.

"Thank you," Maddock said. "How is it that we can understand each other?"

"It is a gift of Eden." Maruti chuckled. "Ironic, really. The peoples of Eden can comprehend another's words, but we do not truly understand one another. I think perhaps we do not want to." He shrugged.

"It's the same where we come from," Spenser said.

Maruti made a clucking sound and wiggled his hand, which seemed to be the Eden version of shaking one's head.

"We are in need of a guide," Maddock said.

"Where do you wish to go?"

"That's the thing. We don't actually know." Maddock paused. He saw no profit in lying to Maruti. "We are looking for the Treasure of Eden. Ever heard of it?"

Maruti stared at the sky for several seconds, then shook his hand. "I have not. Is there another name it might be known by?"

"The Treasure of Lilith, maybe?" Spenser offered. "It's a name I stumbled across in my reading."

The exposed flesh of Maruti's face and palms turned white. He took a step back, paused to catch his breath. He shook both hands vigorously.

"You do not wish to go there. Lilith's temple lies in the middle of Naga territory. They serve her."

"If you won't show us, could you draw us a map?" Maddock pressed.

"I fear it would lead to your death."

"We've already got people trying to kill us," Bones said. "We're hoping if we find the treasure, they'll leave us the hell alone."

"Unless you have her eyes, you will receive no reward. Only death." Maruti looked down at the ground.

"We have one." Maddock wore the eye on a chain around his neck. He took it out and held it up.

Maruti gasped. He gazed at the gem, equal parts terrified and fascinated. He took a few deep breaths, calming himself.

"The man with three blue eyes," he murmured. "Could it be true?"

"Could what be true?" Grizzly asked.

Maruti didn't seem to hear. He gazed at the eye as if hypnotized. "Torn from her once again by the one thing she will never have." He drew in a few sharp, ragged breaths. Finally, he blinked, closed his eyes, and gave his body a shake, as if waking himself up. "I apologize. The spirit sometimes overwhelms us. Another dubious gift of Eden."

"We don't want to cause any trouble for you," Maddock said. "If you will draw us a map, we will be on our way."

"On your own, you have little chance of making it through Naga territory. I will have to guide you. If we are separated, follow the road that leads east."

"How far east?" Bones asked.

"You will know when you get there."

31

Maruti led them off the main path and into the jungle. He picked out trails in the jungle that Maddock could barely see even after they were pointed out to him. Whenever they came close to a Naga village, Maruti would signal for silence by placing his hand over his mouth. Other times, when he felt they were safe, he told them about his people and the land.

Maruti's people were called the Hanuman. He was amused to learn that Hanuman was the monkey king of Hindu lore, and that his own name was another name for the same legendary figure.

The Hanuman, he explained, were one of several peoples who resided in Eden. His people occupied a forested region to the south and east. The Naga lived in the swampy central region, as did the followers of Lilith. Maruti would say no more about Lilith. The entire subject was taboo.

It seemed that many topics were taboo. He said there were lands far away, but he claimed to not know the names of those who resided there. He freely spoke about the Rephaim, giants who lived in the hilly country to the north, but when Maddock asked about the Anakim, another race of giants from Hebrew lore, he made a choking sound, stumbled, and nearly fell.

"Never say that name. If you must speak of them, call them the Stranglers."

He also refused to discuss the Nephilim, although he grudgingly admitted to their existence.

When Bones asked about the Watchers, rock giants associated with the story of Noah, Maruti insisted they change the subject.

"Are we underneath the Earth," Bones asked, "or are

we in an entirely different place?"

"According to our stories, we are both. Our world lies beneath yours, but we exist in a slightly different place. There are only certain locations where…" He paused, thinking hard. "Where the energies of our worlds align. Sometimes these energies are almost identical, but it requires a key, like the eye, to make them as one."

"What are the eyes? Where did they come from?" Maddock asked.

"They were brought from one of the faraway lands by someone of whom I prefer not to speak. They were then stolen by one of your kind, and the owner wanted them back. The treasure is the reward she set aside long ago for the one who returned her eyes."

"I'll settle for half the treasure," Bones said.

"This person you do not wish to discuss," Spenser began, "was she really Adam's first wife?"

"She wanted to be, but he loved another. I will say no more."

"Is Eden the only land beneath the Earth?" Grizzly asked.

"The stories say there are others, some that are a part of your world, and others like ours."

They eventually exhausted the topics Maruti was willing to discuss, and they trudged on in silence. The light above them grew dark and the sky turned azure and then to cobalt. They stopped for food and a brief rest, then continued their trek.

"So, we're just going to walk up to Lilith, hand her the eye, and ask for our reward?" Bones said quietly.

"She's been dead for thousands of years," Maddock said. "My hunch is the eye opens a vault where the treasure is stored."

"She is not dead. She is sleeping."

"We'll be sure not to wake her up, then," Bones said.

Maruti looked like he was about to say more, but then he held his hand to his mouth. Everyone fell silent. He looked around, his protuberant ears twitching.

"There are Naga nearby. Stay here. Do not move until I return." He scurried off into the jungle.

They waited. The minutes ticked by, measured by the pounding of Maddock's heartbeat. He estimated five minutes had passed when they heard a rustling sound.

"About time," Bones whispered. "Wonder where he's been?"

The rustling sound grew louder. It was all around them.

"I don't think that's Maruti," Maddock said.

Tall, dark figures appeared. Lizardmen armed with spears, clubs, and knives. Maddock stopped counting at thirty. Far too many to fight without somebody getting killed. He should never have let Spenser and Grizzly come along.

"Son of a bitch," Bones said. "The little assclown betrayed us."

The largest of the Naga, a tall, broad-shouldered creature with bright green scales, approached. He pointed at Maddock.

"You…" he rasped "come with us."

Maddock saw no other choice. He stood slowly and raised his hands.

"We surrender."

32

The sky was growing lighter as Maddock and the others were herded out of the jungle and into a valley. They followed a weed-choked road lined with flat stones. Maddock had not stopped searching for a way out, but the Naga remained vigilant.

They crested a rise and saw their destination—a stepped, pyramidal tower, like the ziggurats of ancient Babylon. A garden grew atop each level.

"This must be the Temple of Lilith," Bones said. "Looks kind of like the Hanging Gardens of Babylon."

"What's growing up there?" Spenser asked.

Bones squinted. "Looks like fruit trees and flowering plants." He raised his eyebrows. "I think I see beehives."

There were, in fact, huge beehives situated at every corner. Like so many of the creatures that inhabited this world, the bees were giant—each one the size of a hummingbird. They could hear the collective hum from a hundred meters away. Naga tended the gardens, oblivious to the flying insects that buzzed all around them.

As they approached the ceremonial gate that stood just outside the entrance, one of the bees buzzed down and hovered in front of them. Its stripes were metallic gold and iridescent blue.

"It's gorgeous," Spenser said as the creature buzzed away.

Maddock's eyes drifted to one of the beehives and something caught his eye. A pipe led from the bottom of the hive down into the temple.

"Looks like the hives have taps," Grizzly said. "Never heard of a temple that also produced honey."

"Maybe it's not ordinary honey." Maddock was

thinking of the golden substance in Alexander's casket.

Once inside the temple, the group was broken up, and each person led in a different direction. Maddock's first instinct was to fight, but a dozen spears pressed against his body dissuaded him.

"I'll find you," he said to Spenser.

"I know you will." She forced a smile. "Or maybe I'll find you."

Isla sat in a prison cell and stared at the ceiling. The reptilians, called Naga, had chased them down, killed Tama and Hunt, and taken Lark and Isla captive. They had been bathed and dressed in short, belted tunics. The Naga had confiscated the Eye of Alexander. Now they awaited their fate.

"This is not how I expected my life to end," Isla said.

"Relax," Lark said. "We are obviously being prepared to meet Lilith. When she learns we returned the eye, and realizes the extent of our devotion, all will be well."

"If she existed at all, Lilith has been dead since the time of Adam."

"Watch what you say," Lark warned. "Do not speak blasphemy."

Isla closed her eyes, rubbed her temples. There was no talking to Lark.

"I forgive you," Lark said. "It's not your fault. You are a scholar at heart, and you think like one."

"Thank you." Bitterness dripped from Isla's words. She reflected on the choices she had made over the past few years. How her life had changed since the moment she chose loyalty to her family and her people over love. How she had saved Maddock's life and driven him away in the process. If only she had never gotten into bed with the Tuatha.

She heard a woman shouting in English. "It's the twenty-first century. Are we really still objectifying women like this?"

A group of Naga forced a gorgeous woman with long blonde hair and big blue eyes into the cell opposite them. Isla wanted to groan when she saw who it was.

"Oh my goddess," she muttered.

Across the way, Spenser spotted them. "You have got to be kidding me."

Their eyes met and they locked in on one another, neither willing to be the one to look away first.

Lark laughed. "You two look like a couple of gorillas facing off." The two women turned their angry glares on Lark. "Imagine letting a man come between sisters."

"We are not sisters," Isla said.

"All women are sisters. Lilith will teach you."

They were interrupted by a familiar voice.

"You've got to admit, I make this thing look good." A group of Naga escorted Bones into the dungeon. He was clad in a white tunic like those the women wore. They stopped in front of the cells. "You okay?" he said to Spenser.

"I'm fine. The company leaves much to be desired."

Bones turned to see Isla and Lark. His whole demeanor changed.

"Oh. It's the traitor and her friend."

Isla gritted her teeth. Yes, she had stolen a precious artifact from Maddock, but she had a bloody good reason. She could take it no longer. Bones might not believe her, but she would tell the truth nonetheless.

"You and Maddock had been marked for death. I traded the ring and my loyalty for your lives."

"Sure you did," Bones said.

The sound of approaching footsteps filled the passageway. Another group of Naga appeared, escorting Maddock and Grizzly Grant.

"You brought that moron?" Isla pointed at Grizzly.

"At least he's loyal." Bones said.

Maddock refused to look at Isla. He had eyes only for Spenser.

"Don't worry. We're going to get out of this," he assured her.

Isla doubted it. Maddock and Bones were deadly fighters, and Grant could hold his own, but there were far too many Naga to fight them all.

"He looks good in that tunic," Lark whispered. "Perhaps Lilith will let me borrow him."

"Shut up, Lark," Isla muttered.

The Naga unlocked the cells and motioned for the women to exit. They formed up around the captives, a forest of spearpoints aimed at them.

"Wonder where they're taking us?" Spenser said.

"Probably to be sacrificed," Grizzly said. "That's why they cleaned us up first."

"Grant, you're such a ray of sunshine," Isla said.

Grizzly scowled at her and looked away. Isla's shoulders sagged. They all hated her, and she had no one to blame but herself. She had made her choices and now had to live with them.

"Come," one of the Naga said.

"Where are we going?" Lark demanded.

The creature's reply shook Isla to her core.

"We will take you to Lilith."

33

The Naga escorted them to a room at the center of the ziggurat. The walls were lined with finely ground bits of quartz that sparkled where beams of sunlight shone down from the skylights high above. The floor was highly polished marble. Colorful mosaics depicted scenes from nature—reptiles, colorful birds, and flowers in bloom.

"The rest of the place is kind of dingy, but this room is spick-and-span," Bones said.

"Looks like a throne room," Maddock said.

At the far end of the room, steps led up to a marble dais. Upon it sat an ornate wooden throne. Every inch was carved with vines, leaves, and flowers. A serpent adorned each stile, and an owl perched on the top rail.

"The owl and serpent were symbols of Lilith," Lark whispered. No one replied.

They passed by dozens of Naga, most of them unarmed, who had gathered there. They watched in silence as the captives passed by. An air of expectation surrounded them.

"It's like they're waiting for something," Spenser said.

"Maybe they're here to see us get our reward?" Grizzly said.

"More likely they've come to watch our sentencing and execution," Isla said.

"You are all wrong," Lark whispered.

One of their Naga guards prodded her in the back with a bronze knife.

"No talking," it hissed.

The crowd parted and they were confronted by a bizarre creature. The top half of her body resembled that of a human, albeit covered in scales, and the lower half a snake.

The scales of her back were aquamarine, and rippled where the light struck them; those on her belly were light cream in color. She wore a peacock feather headdress shaped like the hood of a cobra. An emerald pendant hung between her breasts. She gazed impassively at them like a snake eyeing a mouse. This would be one of the Ninazu.

"I can't decide if she's hot or not," Bones whispered. He grunted when Spenser elbowed him in the ribs.

"You have returned Lilith's eyes," the Ninazu said.

"We have," Maddock said simply. He was uncertain what was about to happen.

"Who are you?" She sounded disinterested, bored even, as she looked them over.

"We have come to worship the Great Mistress," Lark said.

"All of you. Even this one?" She slithered up to Bones and cupped his chin with the tips of her sharp fingernails. "What sort of human are you?"

"A Cherokee," he said. "What about you? You've got sort of a Quetzalcoatl vibe going on with the feathers."

The assembled Naga erupted. They hissed, stamped their feet, and made slashing motions with their hands. One of the guards poked Bones with a spear. Only the Ninazu appeared unaffected.

"That name is not spoken here. But you are ignorant, so I grant you forgiveness." Her words soothed the angry Naga. "Do you have any more questions, impertinent or otherwise?"

"You got a name?" Bones asked.

"You may call me Nin. My name is easy to pronounce but takes a long time to say."

"What is going to happen to us?" Isla asked.

"That will be for the Great Mistress to decide." Nin slithered to the side and swept her arm back in a regal gesture.

Maddock was stunned by what he saw. At the foot of the steps, directly before the throne, lay a crystal casket filled with golden liquid. There was a shape inside.

"The Great Mistress," she said.

"Hold on." Bones held up his hands. "You're telling me Lilith is inside that casket?"

"I take it that golden liquid is a preservative?" Maddock asked.

"That and more. Eden's honey heals the body, nourishes it. Most important of all, it sustains the tiniest spark of life within that person, so that they can someday be resurrected, stronger than they were before. It is our greatest treasure!"

"Is that the Treasure of Eden? Honey?" Grizzly asked.

"Yes. It is infinitely more valuable than the gold you humans treasure."

"That's the same stuff that was inside Alexander the Great's casket," Grizzly said.

"We call him Alexander the Thief," Nin said.

"Because of the bees and the honeycomb?" Bones asked.

"One of those bees was a queen! That is why he had to be killed. But he had hidden the eyes where we could not find them. Even under the effects of the poison, he remained silent."

"You had Alexander killed?" Maddock asked.

The Ninazu actually cracked a smile. "Not me. We do not live so long as that. But it was done at our command."

Maddock had a suspicious thought." What about Kamehameha? Did you have him killed?"

"I was told the Nightmarchers did it. I do not know why."

"How often do your people drop in on us?" Bones scratched his head. "Are you the ones mutilating all those cattle?"

"We rarely enter your world. Humans are one of the few creatures who foul their own nests. Your air and water are filthy. We prefer not to go there."

"How do you enter? Are there other eyes?" Grizzly asked.

"Lilith has only two eyes. But there are places where we can pass through when conditions are right. On rare occasions it can happen by accident. It is the same for all the peoples of Eden."

"It is time." Nin turned and slithered over to the casket. At her command, the casket lid was removed. Nin clapped her hands twice. Another Ninazu, this one scarlet and yellow with a green headdress, slithered over. She carried a small wooden box.

Nin opened the box, removed the eyes, and held them up for all to see. The Naga hissed softly.

"This is weird," Bones said.

"Great Mistress, I return to you your eyes." Nin reached into the liquid and pulled back the lid of Lilith's left eye to reveal an empty space. With a beatific smile, she pressed one of the eyes into the socket, then did the same with the right eye.

The effect was immediate. Lilith's legs twitched, then her arms. She began to thrash around, spilling honey onto the floor. She sat up and gasped, breathing in air for the first time in thousands of years. She took a few more breaths, then stood.

34

Lilith was strikingly beautiful, with long black, hair and flawless alabaster skin. Her body was lush, with curves that pleased the eye.

"Holy crap," Bones marveled.

Grizzly took an involuntary step forward, unable to tear his eyes away from her. Lark fell to her knees, weeping with joy.

"You guys do see the horns and the tail?" Spenser whispered.

"Men rarely look beyond the breasts," Isla said.

Maddock blinked. Spenser was right. Two short, blood-red horns protruded from her head, and she had a prehensile tail tipped with a sharp, black spike.

"Still hot," Bones said.

Lilith opened her eyes and looked around the hallway. Her smile seemed to lower the temperature by twenty degrees. Wherever she looked, those upon whom she gazed began to shamble toward her like zombies. When she looked away, they paused, puzzled. The effect was Medusa-like.

"Don't look her in the eye," Maddock whispered as her gaze swept toward them.

"Don't worry. I'm not looking at the eyes," Bones said.

"Pig." Isla scowled at him.

"Don't forget, this is all your fault," Bones said. "Screwing us over yet again."

"I'm truly sorry," Isla said. "For everything."

"Humans," Lilith's voice was like a siren's call. "Is Adam among you? Lucifer perhaps? Or the girl?"

"Great Mistress," Nin began, "it has been many thousands of years since you began your sleep.

"A shame." Lilith suddenly paused, cocked her head.

"But you have returned my eyes. You have my thanks."

"Is there a treasure?" Grizzly blurted. "A reward, perhaps?" His voice was dull as if he were not fully in command of his actions.

Lilith's laugh was like a winter gale. "Simple man. There is no reward. It was a fabrication, a fiction crafted by me and spread among your people in the hope that someone would find my eyes and return them."

"Great Mistress, the only reward we seek is to serve you," Lark said, her eyes aglow.

"Actually, I'm not much of a follower," Bones said. "You got the eyes, mission accomplished. We'll see ourselves out."

"You will stay," Lilith said. "The women will serve me. But what to do with the men?" She crooked a finger and Grizzly shuffled over to her. Lilith caressed his cheek. "You are simple. I will use you as a footrest." Grizzly nodded like an obedient puppy, then dropped down on all fours.

"Men are so easy," Isla muttered. Spenser smirked, nodded ruefully.

"Tall man, come to me," Lilith commanded. Bones resisted, then shuffled over to her. His face was twisted into a grimace like the anchor in a game of tug-o-war. "You are stronger than this one, and clever. You will be my fool." With a baleful look on his face, Bones took a seat on the floor a few paces behind her.

Finally, Lilith turned to Maddock, quirked an eyebrow, and inclined her head. Maddock kept his gaze locked in on the center of Lilith's forehead. Still, her gaze was like the tug of gravity. "Come now, don't be shy." Her voice was hypnotic, but Maddock drowned it out by focusing on the song he hated most in the world, the theme song from the movie *Titanic*. Lilith smiled. "You are a stubborn one."

"Tea, bitch," Spenser said reflexively.

"You have no idea," Isla added.

The women exchanged glances, Spenser annoyed, Isla amused.

"You will come to me," Lilith said firmly.

Maddock felt a thousand invisible hands pushing and pulling him in Lilith's direction. He took an involuntary step forward.

"You *are* a strong one, much like Adam. I will enjoy breaking your will." Her gaze hardened. "Kneel before me and kiss my feet."

Again Maddock felt the inexorable pull of her will. He took a halting step, then another. She was winning.

"You will be my consort." Lilith was smiling again. "Our spawn will conquer all the lands of Eden. And then we will turn all of Eden's power upon your own world. Humans aren't good for much, but they make fine livestock. Your meat is stringy but your blood is delicious." She stretched the last word out into a serpentine hiss.

"Great Mistress," Bones said dully. "Can I be your consort? I am literally sitting Indian style for you."

Maddock blinked, Lilith's charisma momentarily washed away by surprise. There was a message in Bones' use of that particular idiom for sitting cross-legged. He was not fully in Lilith's thrall.

"Great Mistress, I would walk five hundred miles to serve you," Isla said.

Maddock almost laughed. Isla was sending a message of her own. The song "I'm Gonna Be" by the Scottish band The Proclaimers was her biggest earworm. Once it got in her head, it took hours to get it out again. That was how she was resisting.

"I would walk five hundred more," Spenser added.

"Enough!" Lilith's voice thundered through the throne room. "You will watch me drink the blood of your friends one by one unless you give yourself to me of your own free will."

"That's not exactly a free choice," Maddock grunted, taking another half-step forward.

"I will start with the one you love the most," Lilith said. "Which one might that be?"

Spenser twitched, struggling to resist the charm of Lilith's voice.

"It is me!" Lark exclaimed. "I love him, but I love you more. Let me serve you."

"You? He could never love one such as you." Lilith sneered at the woman kneeling before her. She leaned down, cupped Lark's chin, and whispered in her ear. "The deeper the devotion, the narrower the mind."

Lark let out a grunt, her eyes went wide. As she gaped at Lilith, blood began to trickle from the corner of her mouth. A black spike jutted out of her back. Lilith's tail had run her through.

Lilith closed her eyes, drew an ecstatic breath, then shoved the dead woman away. She turned her gaze on Isla and Spenser. The women flinched, struggled to look away. Their resolve was crumbling.

"It is one of you two," she said. "The big man is second. But which of you is it? I sense you both care for him."

"It is me," Isla said. "Take me and let them go. I beg you."

"Very well," Lilith said. She wrapped her tail around Isla and pulled her close. "I am famished. It has been a very long time since I dined."

"I will serve you, Mistress," Maddock said.

"No!" Isla and Spenser said in unison.

Lilith looked at him, but did not release Isla.

"Very well. Come, then." Her smile sparkled like a starry sky. Her eyes were twin beacons on a foggy night. A voice whispered in his mind, begging him to serve Lilith, to love her.

Love. He remembered something Maruti had said.

Torn from her once again by the one thing she will never have.

Lilith had tried and failed to seduce Adam. She had power, had worshipers, but did not have what she wanted most. Love was the one thing Lilith would never have.

Torn from her once again...

Her eyes! They had obviously been ripped from their sockets once before. And it was up to him to do it again.

He stumbled forward, held out his hands. He felt her hold on him grow with every step. He would only have one shot at this. He had to hold on. Tears streamed down Spenser's face as Maddock approached Lilith. She reached out with her tail and wrapped it around him.

"This pleases me." She brushed his cheek with the sharp tip of her tail. "But I am still hungry."

Isla let out a gasp as Lilith's fangs pierced her neck. Her eyes met Maddock's, and she mouthed the words, *I love you.* Lilith released Isla and she fell to her knees, her hand pressed to the holes in her neck.

"A little taste for now." Lilith turned to Maddock. "You will serve me?"

"With all my heart." Maddock needed to be convincing. He placed his hands on Lilith's cheeks and firmly pulled her to him. Their lips met. Her presence was overwhelming and nauseating, her scent like cut flowers rotting in a vase. She slipped her forked tongue into his mouth and he wanted to vomit, but he held on. He slipped his right hand down to the small of her back, pulled her close, and she let out a soft note of surprise.

Maddock understood Lilith now. She derived little satisfaction from bending someone to her will. She wanted a man to come to her of his own free will, to choose her the way Adam had chosen Eve over Lilith. He kissed her deeply and felt her relax. With his left hand, he caressed her cheek, then her hair. He felt her tail brush his cheek again.

Lilith broke the kiss. "Tell me you love me," she demanded.

Maddock focused all of his thoughts on Spenser.

"I love you."

Lilith purred like a kitten. So great was her arrogance, her regard for humans so little that she believed Maddock had given in. She cupped his cheek and smiled.

Maddock grabbed the tip of Lilith's tail and drove the spike into her neck.

35

Lilith let out a scream of pure pain that rose to a shriek of abject terror when Maddock thrust his thumbs into her eye sockets and tore the Eyes of Alexander free. She flung Maddock away. Pain shot through him when he struck the marble floor. Lilith let out another shriek.

And then chaos reigned.

Many of the Naga broke and ran, but others closed in on the humans, determined to protect their Mistress. Maddock spotted Bones in the middle of the crowd, bobbing and weaving like a boxer. Each crisp punch he threw struck a Naga square on the nose and sent it slumping to the ground.

Grizzly had recovered his wits and wrested a spear from one of the guards. He stabbed a Naga in the throat, turned, and drove the butt of his spear into another's face.

Tears streaming down her face, Nin had picked up Lilith and was carrying her back to her casket.

Maddock looked around for Spenser and saw her helping Isla toward the door. Naga closed in on them on both sides.

Maddock clambered to his feet and ran to their aide. He drove his shoulder into a Naga and sent it crashing into a crowd of its fellows, knocking them all to the ground. He turned and drove his fist into the face of another. As it fell, he snatched the spear from its lifeless hands, turned, and impaled another.

The Naga were terrible fighters and not very robust, but there were far too many of them to fight against in this confined space.

"Make for the door!" he shouted.

Bones and Grizzly broke off their individual battles and

made a beeline to Maddock, who was fighting to keep the Naga off Spenser and Isla. Each clutched a spear and was covered in cuts and bruises.

"How about we cut a path through these assclowns?" Bones growled.

"Let's do it," Maddock said. The Naga were numerous, but weak. The three men formed up in front of Spenser and Isla, and charged. The Naga resistance crumbled as the humans fought their way to freedom.

They battled along through a series of narrow corridors. But every time they believed they had broken themselves free, more Naga appeared. Finally, they paused for a rest.

"I'm exhausted." Grizzly leaned on his spear, catching his breath. "We have got to find a way out soon."

"Fighting the Naga is easy," Bones said. "But it's like harvesting a field of wheat by hand. It's too big a job for a handful of guys. And women," he added for Spenser's benefit.

In the distance, they heard hissing and running feet. The Naga were closing in again. Maddock wondered how much fight he and his friends had left in them, and how much farther Isla could make it.

"How is Isla doing?" Maddock asked.

"Still alive, but she's weak." The expression on Spenser's face was one of despair. "We need to find a way out of here soon."

"Perhaps I can help with that."

They turned to see Maruti standing in the doorway.

"I thought you ditched us," Bones said.

"I tried to lead the Naga away from you, but I failed," Maruti said. "This is the first chance I have had to get inside the temple. Follow me."

He guided them back the way they had come, up one level, and out onto one of the terraces that ringed the ziggurat. Giant bees buzzed all around.

"Come on," the little simian said. "They are no danger to us."

As he had predicted, the bees went about the business of producing the honey that was Eden's greatest treasure, and paid no mind to the intruders among them.

They ran down a ramp and onto the clear land that surrounded the ziggurat. The jungle loomed a hundred meters away. The hisses and cries of the Naga filled the air.

"We must get to the trees," Maruti said.

"Damn! They spotted us!" Bones said.

Maddock glanced over his shoulder. At least a hundred Naga were hot on their trail. Spenser and Isla would never make it in time.

"Grizzly, help me with Isla," he said. "Spenser, you make a run for it."

"Bullshit," she said. "Give me that spear and I'll cover your back." She lowered her voice. "I won't go home without you."

Damn the stubborn woman. He handed over his spear, then he and Grizzly draped Isla's arms over their shoulders and began to run.

The jungle seemed to hang on the horizon like a mirage, growing no closer. The Naga closed in.

"On your right!" Spenser shouted.

Maddock and Grizzly veered left. A spear zipped past Maddock's head and stuck in the ground.

"Thanks!" he said.

They kept running.

Maddock's breath came in gulps. His legs felt like water, his arms were sandbags. The rigors of their search were catching up to him. Isla was unconscious, dead weight, the tips of her toes dragged the ground.

"Almost there!" Bones shouted.

"We're not going to make it," Spenser said.

Maddock heard a twanging sound like a guitar string snapping. An arrow flew from high in the trees and struck a Naga in the chest. And then a discordant symphony rang out as dozens of archers let fly. The arrows flew like a swarm of hornets, shredding the Naga charge. The reptilians faltered. Another volley broke them completely.

When they reached the jungle, they paused to catch their breath.

"My people," Maruti explained. "When you were captured, I sought their help."

"Thank you," Maddock gasped. "The reinforcements arrived was just in the nick of time."

"Lilith's eyes, did you take them back again?"

The eyes! In the chaos and confusion, Maddock had forgotten all about them. He felt something heavy in his pocket, reached in, and scooped out the two orbs.

"You truly are the man with three blue eyes." Maruti pointed at Maddock's eyes, and to the blue stone in his palm.

"We've got the eyes. How do we get home again?"

"Go east," Maruti said. "We will keep the Naga at bay."

36

They came to a pathway in the jungle and followed it east. They kept eyes and ears peeled for the Naga, but it seemed they had outdistanced their pursuit. Maruti had repaid his life debt to Maddock and then some.

The air was cooler here. Birds sang, and beams of sunlight filtered down onto the path. They spotted trees they actually recognized—apple and pear trees heavy with fruit.

Isla was suffering from the effects of Lilith's bite. Her breathing was shallow, her pulse weak. They were losing her.

"There's nothing we can do for her," Spenser said. "If only we had some of Eden's honey."

"We don't," Maddock said. "We'll just have to keep on going."

The light was beginning to fade when they came to a walled garden. The gate was open, so they went inside.

"Whoa!" Bones breathed.

The garden was filled with the most lifelike sculptures Maddock had ever seen. Creatures of Eden, animals both familiar and exotic, even humans were crafted in lifelike detail.

The grass beneath their feet was soft and lush. Everything here was calm and peaceful. Isla appeared to sense it too. Her eyes fluttered open for a second and she smiled before passing out again.

They followed a cobblestone path that wound through the garden until they reached the center. There, lying on a stone pedestal, were the shattered remains of what had once been a sculpture of a giant apple.

"Who are you? What are you doing in my garden?"

The voice thundered inside Maddock's head, made his ears ring. The others flinched too. He turned to see a bearded giant clad in a robe, stalking toward them. In his right hand he held a flaming sword.

"What the hell is that?" Bones said.

"I suppose it's one of the cherubim who were set to guard the…" Maddock suddenly understood. "We've found it! This is the garden God made in the East of Eden."

"Great," Bones said. "We find the Garden of Eden only to be killed by Hagrid."

The giant man drew closer, and he hesitated. His expression softened.

"Humans from Earth," he said. "I have not seen your like in more years than I can remember." He suddenly became aware of his burning sword. The fire went out and he sheathed it. "Forgive me. I forgot I was carrying it."

"We didn't mean to trespass," Spenser said. "Our friend needs help."

The giant man frowned, then knelt beside Isla. "I sense Lilith's venom inside of her."

"Lilith bit her on the neck," Maddock said. "Can you help her?"

The man grimaced, let out a rumbling sigh. "I can save her life, but I cannot stop the change."

"What change?" Bones asked.

"Lilith is a demon. Your friend will begin to turn. It is a small bite, so she might not become a full demon. But she will no longer be human."

"Can she come back with us?" Spenser asked.

"No. But she may remain here in Eden. We will care for her."

They waited while the man tended to Isla. He gave them and drink, and sat with them while they rested.

"Thank you for your help," Maddock said.

"You are welcome."

"By the way, we didn't break your apple." Bones pointed at the broken sculpture.

"Oh, that thing." The man's laughter rolled like thunder. "It has been broken since Lilith was a girl. She and her friends were playing in the garden and they broke it. I'm afraid I lost my temper. Chased them out of the garden with my flaming sword, told them never to come back." He chuckled. "Of course, they came back the very next day. Scoundrels, the lot of them?"

"Are you talking about Adam and Eve?" Spenser asked.

"Adam, Eve, Lilith, and Lucifer."

"Lucifer? The fallen angel?" Maddock asked.

"He was no angel, but he was a good boy. The cleverest Naga I ever met. His mind was as keen as any." The man shook his head. "It is a sad thing what happened between them."

"Could you tell us the story?" Spenser asked.

"It's a story as old as time. Lucifer loved Eve, Lilith loved Adam. Neither got what they wanted. Lucifer remained their friend, wanting to be close to Eve any way he could.

"Lilith could not take the rejection. She left our land on a quest for a legendary dark power."

"The eyes?" Maddock asked.

"Yes." The man nodded sadly. "She returned changed. Her new eyes gave her the ability to enthrall, but they came at a price. It twisted her very nature."

"She traded her humanity for the power to control others?" Spenser asked. "Sounds like a lot of people I know."

"To her surprise, the eyes had little effect on Adam, so great was his devotion to Eve. It was then Lilith resorted to blackmail. She vowed to murder Eve if Adam did not choose her."

"What happened?" Grizzly asked.

"Adam went to Lilith, convinced her he loved her, and then he stole her eyes and returned home to find Eve." A shadow passed over his face.

"I take it there's not a happy ending?" Spenser asked.

"Adam did not warn Eve of his plan. She believed Adam had set her aside in favor of Lilith. Heartbroken, Eve sought comfort in the arms of Lucifer. She and Adam forgave one another, and to protect them from Lilith's vengeance, I sent them to your world."

"I sense a twist," Bones said.

"Lilith was pregnant with Lucifer's child. They named him Cain and Adam raised him as his own. But Cain had the same jealous nature as his father, and the target of his envy was his younger brother, Abel."

"We know how the story ends," Bones said. "Cain killed Abel and was made to wander the Earth."

"Wrong. He was sent back to Eden, where he lived out his days among the Naga." The man gazed at the sky for a few seconds, then stood.

"It is time to send you home," he said brightly.

Maddock frowned. A part of him wanted to remain here in this garden of serenity. But he knew he could never be happy in such a place. Yes, he was safe and at peace, but what else was there? How many times could someone walk around the same garden, look at the same trees and flowers, eat the same food, talk with the same people? He wanted more. And he could not get that here.

"What do we need to do?" Maddock said.

"The three of you follow me."

The big man led them through the garden. Maddock soaked in the sight, sounds, and smells, somehow knowing his senses would never have an experience like this again. They passed a gazebo where Isla slept atop pile of soft blankets. She looked thin, drained. Maddock hesitated.

"You must not wake her," the man said. "All will be explained when she wakes."

"In spite of all the things she did, I still feel guilty about leaving her behind," Spenser said. "If she hadn't spoken up, taken my place, it would be me you were leaving behind."

"If that were the case, we'd both be staying."

"You two make me sick," Bones said. "It's all just too sweet. I'm talking, romantic-comedy-level."

"Shut up, Bones. I'm dealing with something here," Spenser said.

"You saved Isla's life by getting her out of Lilith's temple when you had every reason to leave her behind. Your debt is paid," Maddock said.

Spenser smiled sadly, gave Maddock's hand a squeeze. "Thank you."

They halted before a statue of a bearded, two-faced man. In one hand he held a staff, in the other, a key. Maddock recognized him at once.

"That's the Greco-Roman god Janus," he said. In mythology, Janus was the god of doorways, gates, and transitions.

"That is one of many names by which he is known. Now, each of you place your hand on his key. There is no need to grip it. To touch it is enough."

Maddock and his friends touched the key. He felt a tingling sensation that raced up his arm and spread out across his body. He glanced at Spenser, who forced a smile.

"See you on the other side," Grizzly said hoarsely.

"Any chance you could drop us off in Vegas?" Bones asked.

The man spoke a single word in a language Maddock could never hope to comprehend. It was musical, resonant, and harsh at the same time.

A cool breeze swept through the garden. It swirled around them until they were inside a vortex. The tingling sensation grew stronger. Something was happening. His eyes met those of the giant, and he summoned the courage to ask the question he had been dying to ask.

"Are you God?" he shouted.

"Me?" the man replied, a sly grin on his face. "I am a simple gardener."

37

Maddock felt a jolt, and then an icy cold surrounded him. He opened his eyes and immediately felt the burn of salt water. Where in the hell had the so-called Gardener sent them?

He looked around. Bones was swimming for the surface. Spenser and Grizzly were a few meters below him. He signaled to them, but they were swimming in opposite directions. In dark water like this, it could be difficult to tell which way was up. Maddock blew out and watched the bubbles float up toward the surface.

He swam over to Spenser, grabbed her by the ankle. When she looked back, he pointed up. She nodded and swam for the surface. Bones spotted her and swam back to give her a hand while Maddock went after Grizzly.

By the time he caught up with his friend, his lungs burned from lack of oxygen. He got his friend oriented in the proper direction and the two swam with all their might. Maddock saw a glimmer of light. The surface was tantalizingly close but seemed to hang just out of reach.

Grizzly was struggling, growing frantic as he fell behind. Maddock grabbed him by the belt and towed him along. The added weight slowed him down.

He saw spots in front of his eyes and his field of vision narrowed. His chest cramped. *I'm going to run out of air*, he thought as his sight faded. A shadow appeared at the corner of his eye.

When he came to again, he was sitting on the deck of a boat, vomiting up a mouthful of sea water. He looked around for his friends. They were all safe.

"That was nasty." A tall, muscular man with deep

umber skin smiled down at him. Behind him stood a tall, tanned man with brown hair and a short, red-haired man slathered in sunscreen. It was his crew! Willis Sanders, Matt Barnaby, and Corey Dean. Willis and Matt were clad in wetsuits.

"What are you guys doing here?" Maddock said.

"You can thank Tam Broderick and the Professor," Corey said. "Tam thought it would be a good idea to stake out all the places Professor identified as portals to wherever the hell you all went."

"You found us just in time," Maddock said. "Where are we, exactly?"

"Red Sea, baby!" Matt proclaimed. "Right where you always said it would be."

Maddock smiled, nodded. He was too weary to feel much sense of triumph.

"I still can't believe it happened," Spenser said. "It was real, wasn't it?"

Maddock felt something press against his thigh. He dug into his pocket, took out two perfectly round gems, and held them up to the light.

"These look real enough," he said. "No idea what to do with them now."

"The Eyes of Alexander." Spenser sighed. "Dane Maddock, you certainly do make my life interesting."

The End

ABOUT THE AUTHOR

David Wood is the USA Today bestselling author of the action-adventure series,the *Dane Maddock Adventures*, and many other works. He also writes fantasy under his David Debord pen name and science fiction as Finn Gray. He's a member of International Thriller Writers and the Horror Writers Association. David and his family live in Santa Fe, New Mexico. Visit him online at www.davidwoodweb.com and get a free reader's guide to the Dane Maddock universe and his other works.

Printed in Great Britain
by Amazon